Praise for Vee James'

The Little Ship of Horrors

From beginning to finish, the story was well done. I realize this is a rendition of a popular horror-comedy-romance tale, but it is still refreshing and different. This is a book I would recommend to anyone who enjoys sci-fi, romance, comedy, horror and fun in general!

—Charla White

I am a fan of the original Little Shop of Horrors, and this iteration is just as good. The dialogue is absolutely fantastic and seeing Chuck turn from a meek janitor into a (somewhat) confident - well, I won't say what because that would be a spoiler, so we'll go with person - person is wonderful.

Chief Roswell is the perfect security officer/investigator for dealing with the situation - or, rather, for mucking up the situation while Chuck and Violet actually handle it.

*And the transporter? It is just.... **chef's kiss***
All in all, a wonderful read.

—Jennifer C.

Big fan of the original and this adaptation does its job so well. We find our heroes in a fantastic setting created by someone both well acquainted with sci-fi and the original story who ties them together in a lighthearted fun read.

—Daniel

Definitely a cute rendition on the romantic comedy horror story. Think some of my favorite parts is the banter between Chuck and the Transporter. This was a fun read.

—Bable2QT

Also by Vee James

The Chronicles of Neccabashar
Neccabashar
Neccabashar: the Sequel

The Witch's Cookbook: A Tale of Faerie

Ancient World Horrors: A collection of Short Horrors

Visit me at *www.veejames.com*
Or send me a note at *veejamesauthor@gmail.com*

THE LITTLE SHIP OF HORRORS

BY

VEE JAMES

Notice: This is a work of fiction. Names, characters, places, incidents, and historical references are the products of the author's imagination or are used fictitiously and are not to be construed as real. Any resemblance to actual events, locales, organizations, or persons, living or dead, is entirely coincidental.

Rare Image Publications
From the Crow's Nest Studio
21013 Timber Ridge Terrace, #301
Ashburn, Va. 20147

Cover Illustration by Carmen Amato
Book Formatting by pen2publishing.com

ISBN: 978-1-7349772-4-0

First edition published: January 2020

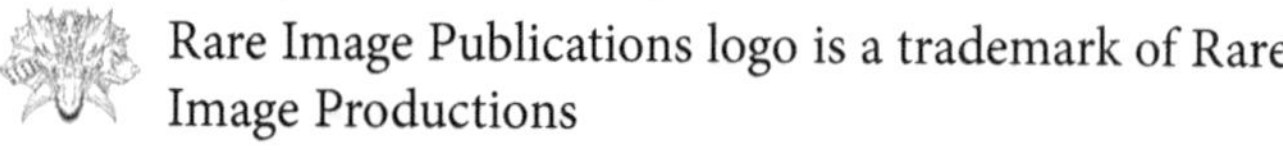

Visit us at www.veejames.com

This book is dedicated in loving memory to the sweet and funny soul of Douglas Noel Adams, author of "The Hitchhiker's Guide to the Galaxy" series as well as sometime script editor of the "notorious" (his word) Dr. Who television series. I wish I could have had tea with him.

THE LITTLE SHIP OF HORRORS

BY VEE JAMES

Table of Contents

Chapter One

"Nice Bumping into You"

There are objects that drift slowly through space, riding the eddies of gravitational forces for billions of slow, uneventful years. There are others, comets being a good example, that speed quickly along, driven by the heavy gravity of a star. And there are still others that tear through the vastness of space at unimaginable speed, coming so near the speed of light as to make their very existence a question to any observer.

"Did you see that?"

"What?"

"Oh, never mind. I thought I saw something."

You know, that sort of thing.

But our attention is now drawn to a different kind of object; one that does not rely on gravity alone to push or pull it across space's great distances. Instead, the object is a space-going vessel, an enormous space liner, using its own power source, directed by calculations of speed and distance programmed into various computers. Engines thrusting, retros firing, and people (yes, people), giving orders, plotting courses, and making adjustments.

This craft, this marvel of man's intellect, is a huge space-going passenger liner, moving along a path seen only by the humans and their computers. The invisible line is a calculated course through the vast emptiness. For, you see, this ship has a mission: it has to *be* somewhere. That is, it has to be somewhere other than where it is now – and soon.

Far down inside the craft, past the luxury decks, below the saunas and pools, many decks beneath the five-star dining rooms, bars, casinos, and gymnasiums, down one non-descript hallway reserved for crew persons' cabins, and just inside one short, dreary passage, are the quarters of a janitor, a maintenance engineer by the exact entry in the ship's records, one Charles Trumbo ("Chuck" to his few friends).

At this moment, Chuck is asleep and dreaming aboard this majestic ship enroute to distant vacation destinations. The janitor, however, is not on vacation but is an employee of the owners of the great ship, the Dwarf Star Cruise Company, currently off his shift, fast asleep and dreaming.

The subject of his dream is the most common and frequent subject of all his dreams. Not that he has such varied resources to draw on for dream material. After all, his waking life consists mostly of making sure that the floors in his assigned sections are clean and the trash and disposal shafts stay cleared all the way through the massive ship, down to the giant ZAP Disposer Unit (Zap-DU, for short) in the belly of the stately ship. His most critical and technical function is the twice-weekly pushing of four buttons in an exact and slightly demanding sequence, activating the monstrous Zap-DU's garbage ejection sequence. But since there is usually at least one superintendent janitor looking over his shoulder when he does this, there is little chance for error anyway.

Nevertheless, Chuck looks forward to this assignment and the powerful feeling it gives him to activate the huge disposal machine.

Dreaming as he is now, his imagination puts him in command, not just of the ship's disposer unit but of the entire spaceliner.

"All systems are GO for docking, Captain," calls one of the crew.

There stands Captain Chuck at the helm of this magnificent ship, wearing the very sophisticated blue dress cap and gold-trimmed jacket of a captain of the Dwarf Star Cruise Company, his hands gripping the control wheel, steering the massive craft into the dock of Janus 12, the largest deep space colony in existence.

"Beginning docking maneuver," Chuck calls out to his crew.

All onboard hold their collective breaths as he guides the ship into the enormous slip with no room to spare…a perfect docking job.

In his dream, it is always a perfect docking job, and the crew and passengers always erupt in enthusiastic cheers, looking up at him in awe from the lower deck and heaping their praises upon him. The communication panel on the bridge buzzes and an orderly hands him the receiver. No surprise, it's the Admiral calling to congratulate him and invite him up to tea. The dream ends the same way every time. Just as he is about to receive a congratulatory kiss from the admiring Admiral's daughter, the time-date console next to his bunk, scientifically designed to bring the mind of a sleeping human to full waking consciousness in seven-tenths of a second, ejects him from his bed (and his dream) so forcefully that he finds himself kissing the wall of his tiny cabin.

Wha—? he thinks, then sighs, pushing away from the wall. *No use going back to sleep now. I might just as well get up.*

The dreary realization that he still is, and may always be, a janitor comes flooding back into his thoughts, the same place so recently occupied by the grand and glorious feeling of command and respect. The only consolation for him is that today just happens to be the day that he is scheduled to go down to the Zap-DU and activate the huge machine.

The time-date console reminds him that he has only twenty-one minutes to get to the Maintenance Disposer Section.

As he hurries through the long halls toward the transporter elevators, he thinks about his dream.

It's a fool's wish, isn't it? he thinks, But aren't all dreams? Still, to steer the ship even once would give me such a thrill. Chuck sighs deeply as he falls into the daydream version of his favorite dream, speeds around a corner, and runs headlong into a young lady in a scientist's uniform.

"Oof!"

"Oh!"

"Oh my!"

"Oops!"

"I've got it. Whoa!"

They tumble in a heap, he landing in a sprawl and she plopping down on her rather shapely bottom and dropping an armload of small packages.

There is the momentary shock and the requisite struggling to the feet, his hurried embarrassed apologies, both of them quite flushed and both oddly excited by this brief contact with someone outside of their solitary existences.

"I'm quite sorry, really," Chuck says.

"You should watch where you're going," she snaps.

"Terribly, terribly sorry. Here let me help you with those."

"I can manage just fine by myself."

"I'm sorry. I wasn't watching. Here's one more. "

Chuck is unexpectedly stunned into speechless awe by the greenest eyes he has ever seen. Never mind that they are shining with a fierceness no man should have to face. All Chuck can see is their beauty.

She snatches the package, gives him one last glare, turns and marches off down the corridor.

He calls out to her, "Nice…um…bumping into you."

"*Hmpf*," she hmpfs.

Note: This young lady in the scientist's uniform is, indeed, a scientist. She is, in fact, the same cute botanist we will meet again later in the story, as will our janitor.

With face still a little red with embarrassment both at his clumsiness and his close encounter with the pretty girl, Chuck enters the transport elevator.

"What deck, please?" chirps the mechanical voice of the transporter.

"Maintenance Disposer Section, please."

The transporter unit remains in place, and after a moment, Chuck repeats his request a little louder, "The, ah, Maintenance Disposer Section?"

"What deck, please," comes the terse reply.

"Oh, um, lower deck 143."

The transporter's doors slam shut and the unit jerks into motion. The numbers of the decks they pass are displayed on the bright yellow transporter display: 29…27…25…

"Deck 24," the transporter announces, and the unit comes to a halt. The doors whisk open, and a couple of civilian workers get on. "What deck, please?"

"Well," chortles one, "That's not what Johnson said."

"No?" asks the other.

"No, he said-"

"What deck, please," asks the transporter in a friendly but insistent tone.

The man looks up, "Oh, sorry, Pharmacology, deck 20. So anyway, he said he didn't give a drip what happened. They could do as they pleased with the thing but if he had to look at it another minute, he was going to turn it into space dust."

They both laugh at this until teardrops form in their eyes. "God, that Johnson is such a wanker."

"Deck 20."

The doors open and two female administration workers stand aside to let the men out.

"What did Smythe say?" asks the second man as he gets off.

The women get on.

"He said, 'Let him. I'll see he pays for it with his-"

The doors close. "What deck, please?"

Chuck is a bit overwhelmed by a perfume one of them is wearing and sneezes. The women take no notice.

"So," says one woman, "Why don't we just go in and tell her?"

"Deck 18, please." The transporter begins to move. "Oh no, my dear. Heavens, you must be joking. You know how sensitive she is."

"Well, someone's got to tell her. We can't just let her go around like that."

"Not me, I can tell you that."

"Well, someone…a friend…should let her know."

"Fine dear, then you can do that if you want to. Just don't let on it came from me."

The second woman hesitates. "Is it, you know, obvious?"

The first one giggles, "Like a coconut on the tip of a straw." They both laugh heartily.

"Deck 18." The doors whisk efficiently open.

"Well then," the second one says thoughtfully, "She must see it every morning in the mirror."

They get off the transporter. "Honey, if I had one, I'd make sure my foundation covered it up."

The doors close and our janitor is finally alone on the transporter, but the unit doesn't move.

"Transporter?" says Chuck.

"What deck, please?"

"What deck? I told you when I got on."

"What deck, please?"

"Oh, for goodness sake," Chuck snorts violently, "Lower deck 143, the Maintenance Disposer Section, as I told you before. Please hurry."

In a testy voice, the elevator says, "No need to get snippy with me."

"What?" says our incredulous janitor, "What did you say?"

The mechanical voice sighs, "You heard me. There's no need to get snippy with me. I'm doing *my* job."

"Well, if I don't get to the Maintenance Disposer Section pretty damn soon, they'll accuse me of not doing mine."

The transporter passes the midline deck and continues down through the lower decks. …21…36…47…

The transporter hums along in silence for several minutes then slows.

"What's going on? Why are we slowing down?"

"I'm receiving a top priority message." Chuck hears several small tones followed by a series of scritchy-scratchy beeps and dot-dash sounds. The transporter comes to a halt so suddenly our friend is practically thrown through the floor. Then the transporter begins to zoom straight up at a terrific speed.

"Oh. What? What?" cries Chuck, "Where are you going?"

"Priority call," replies the transporter, "Sorry, Mac."

"What?"

"Priority call. The military needs my services jo-jo."

"What? Jo-jo?"

"Right now, immediately, on-the-double."

"Look," Chuck pleads, "Couldn't you just take me first and then go back for them?"

"And lose my permit? Not a chance, guy."

Our janitor fumes, "You're supposed to serve *me*. You were built to do what *I* say. And I say, 'Take me to Lower 143 right now.'"

The transporter continues to head straight up, the indicator showing the floors they are passing 28…36…45…

"Do you hear me?" shouts the incensed janitor, "I said right—"

The lift screeches to a halt and the doors fly open.

"-now!" he screams.

Seven young space military cadets stand there, staring at him. Each has the same identical youthful sneer on his or her face. Each looks around the interior of the transporter and back to him. A couple of them suppress small giggles and then one of them finally speaks up, "Okay, daddy-o, whatever you say." They break out in laughter and pile jauntily into the transporter. It gets pretty tight what with their helmets, flight bags, and crew cuts. The transporter instantly smells like a locker room after the big game.

"What deck, sir," the elevator asks snappily.

"Sub three forward," pipes up one of them.

"Yes sir," answers the transporter sharply. The doors click efficiently shut and the unit whisks them forward.

"Sub three forward?" the janitor asks weakly.

"Yep," one of the smiling faces answers, "Weapons pods. Hooah!"

And then, all together, they let loose their war cry, "Hooah!"

Our janitor, jammed into the rear of the transporter with a helmet pressed firmly against his ribs, slumps against the rear wall, outnumbered and beaten. He suffers quietly until they arrive at the weapons deck and the cadets swagger off.

The doors of the transporter close but the unit doesn't move.

"Well?" says the janitor testily.

"What deck, please?"

"Don't start that with me."

"Oh, you again?"

"Get me to the Maintenance Disposer Section. I've only got three minutes."

The transporter lurches into motion and lets out a mechanical sniff, "You wouldn't hear our boys in blue whining like that."

"Leave me alone."

"I'm just saying," the Transporter says wistfully, "Ah, what I wouldn't give to be one of them…"

"Oh, shut up."

The display counts the decks: Lower deck…42…60…73…90…125…139…141…142…

The transporter suddenly lurches, coughs, and then grinds to a halt. The doors shudder open.

"I have a maintenance problem," the Transporter announces.

"What? But we're almost there. We're only one deck away."

"I have a maintenance problem," continues the Transporter, "And I must shut down." The lights in the transporter slowly dim.

The janitor sputters with almost hysterical frustration, "You can't…you can't do this. I'll be late."

"Better run," says the Transporter, "I am now Out-of-Order." The lights go out and the unit becomes silent as a grave.

One very angry janitor emerges from the transporter hurling invectives at the pugnacious machine and runs off for the stairs in an attempt to not be too late for work. He doesn't hear the transporter's smug retort that the next time it might forget to open the door. Chuck doesn't catch the wry mechanical laugh as the unit switches itself back on, turns on the lights, smoothly closes the doors, and heads off to the luxury decks. It's had enough slumming for one day.

If Chuck is still mad after his long run to the Maintenance Disposer Section, his supervisor's attitude is no consolation. A burly man whose vast stomach reveals years of supervising instead of doing, the boss berates Chuck for his late arrival, talking to him like you might scold a small puppy who has just soiled your best cardigan. He refuses to listen to the janitor's "the transporter had it in for me" story and orders Chuck to "get this thing over with because it stinks to high heaven down here" and he wants to get back to his maintenance supply inventory (short for "taking a nap behind the stacks of storage"). The boss also points out the janitor can get back to swabbing the decks.

Several minutes later, the pushing of the first three buttons of the Garbage Ejection Sequence has proceeded normally and Chuck is waiting for the order to be given to push the last button and complete the job. As the huge machine grinds the trash and rubbish to a pulp, the janitor starts to daydream again. (Look, he can't help it; it's a bloody boring job.)

Once again, he's the Captain of the great vessel, this time waiting for the enemy ship to move within blaster range so he might push the button which fires the trans-phasors and sends the bastards to Davey Jones' AirLocker.

An insistent beep calls the supervisor, and the man turns away for a moment to answer his communicator. The janitor stands with finger poised over the last button, only half-aware of what is going on around him. The Zap-DU finishes the grinding sequence and our daydreaming friend, lulled by the monotone drone of his supervisor's voice, proceeds to press down on Button Four without another thought.

The point should be made clear that Chuck has done absolutely nothing wrong. Nothing. If he had waited, he would have heard the supervisor finish his call and order him to proceed. The supervisor might even have said something like "What are you waiting for?" or some such similar thing.

Neither our friend nor his supervisor could possibly know that the gigantic arms of the Zap-DU would stop in mid-motion and the entire operation, the normally flawless ejection of ground garbage into space would, for the first time in the operational history of the whole Titan-class Star Rover series, come to a complete halt. And no one onboard could possibly have guessed that the maintenance crews would, two hot and sweaty hours later, find something lodged in a critical place in the arm assembly, jamming-up the entire works.

But almost anyone with half a brain could guess who gets the blame for the entire incident.

Chapter Two

A Violet, By Any Other Name...

Mixed in with the grease and dust around the arm's gears, the engineers finally pry a fist-sized rock out of its tight spot. The engineers marvel at the incredible strength of this relatively small rock and discuss studying the thing in their workshop. The scientists overhear the engineers talking and decide that they really should have the first crack at studying it in their lab, being scientists and all. The Head Maintenance Supervisor overhears the scientists arguing with the engineers and announces that the Maintenance Department will be keeping the rock as they're the ones who found it. A few other minor science departments, the metallurgists, the geologists, and the tectonisists get involved and pretty soon a vicious political war breaks out.

Flaming e-mails fly and Captain Richard Cable, interrupted during an important session with his manicurist, is suddenly overwhelmed with communications coming from all over the ship. At first, he thinks the hull has been breached by space pirates. He orders a full alert and weapons deployment, which thrills the cadets to no end but terrifies several hundred passengers for whom, until this morning, the biggest conflict of their day was which cocktail to order next.

As red lights flash and klaxons scream, the Captain is told the real nature of the "emergency". No pirates, no breach of the hull, just a hissy fit between a bunch of wimpy digit brains who have nothing better to do than argue over a rock.

Being the decisive type, Captain Cable shows his mettle. In order to solve the argument between these pencil-necks and make sure that this matter doesn't take up any more of his time, he orders his secretary to print out the name of every science, engineering, and maintenance department on the ship and put them into a fighter pilot's helmet. With multiple conference screens squeezing in from all sides, he draws the name of the department that will get to examine the rock first. He draws the Botany Department. There is a cry of disbelief, but the captain will hear none of their complaints.

"Get back to work," he screams, "And don't bother me again unless space pirates are breaching the hull."

The minutes of the meeting are emailed all around and that is that. Well, not quite. The Botany department director, an unimportant man suddenly thrust into a very important position, sends his junior scientist to pick up the rock while he plays political football with the other department heads. By the end of the negotiation, he's been able to obtain an extra two weeks paid leave, three bottles of Wolf Whiskey, and a classic copy of "Arias of the Second Dawning" from the head of the Geology department, who will pick up the rock the next morning and sneak it off to his department for a real going over.

So, here comes our cute botanist back into the picture as promised. Her name, apropos for a botanist, is Violet and she has been assigned to pick up the rock and transport the thing to the Botany Lab. A military escort, two big meatheads in perfect uniforms, wait for her as she arrives in the Maintenance Disposer Section.

As she trundles her little cart back toward the Botany department, the meathead guards march in lockstep behind her. Violet sees her girlfriend, Kate, a cute dental hygienist who happens to be in the science wing dropping off some images at the digital processing center.

"Hi, Kate." Violet can't believe her friend's perfect smile.

"Hi, Violet." Kate can't believe the taller meathead guard who gives her an "I know what you're thinking" look.

"So, Kate, what's going on?"

"Violet, you've got to come up to the Saturn Café tonight. You know that guy I told you about? You know, Tom, the drilling and exploration guy with the chest like a Berber rug? Well, his band is playing there tonight. It's going to be crazy!" While Violet is taking this in, Kate shoots an "I know you know what I'm thinking" look back at the leering guard.

Violet considers, "Upper Deck Fifteen?"

"Sixteen. And don't bring anybody. I want you to meet Silvio, Tom's friend."

Violet glances back at the guards and catches the taller one giving Kate an "I don't care if you know, I just want to do you" look.

"I'd better go. The boss wants this rock examined right away."

"Okay, sweetie. We're all meeting at nine."

"Okay, I'll come up. Ta-ta."

"Bye, Violet." Kate shoots a "Looks like you missed your chance" look at the big guard and turns to leave before he can give his "Next time for sure, babe" look.

Thirteen minutes later, Violet and her bodyguards reach the Botany Lab.

"Thanks, guys, I can take it from here."

"Yes, ma'am," says the taller one as he gives her a "You're hotter than your friend if you want to give it a go" look.

"Have a nice night," says Violet, returning his look with a "Not on your life, Buster" look of her own.

The research lab in which Violet works is a verdant green place with gardens growing in such profusion as to make even earth-bound green thumbs simply…er, well green with envy, so to speak. Azaleas, hyacinths, and irises of all colors grow next to cacti, desert roses, water plants, and that's just on her desk.

She locks the little cart containing the rock specimen into the bay of the examining table, switches the power on, and busies herself tending to some recently bloomed crocuses. She wanders off to check on those new purple orchids she's been nursing back to health.

The botanical analysis computer scoffs at being asked to do a complete analysis on a rock. It's a botany computer for Gawd's sake, not some kind of mineral miner's quad-corder. But the human isn't really paying attention, so the botanical analysis computer reluctantly begins its analysis.

What's this? The machine becomes slightly intrigued. There are patterns on the rock surface unlike anything the examining computer has seen before…or, rather, maybe like something buried deep down in its memory banks. It searches the rather extensive, if rarely used, geological files but these patterns do not match any geological data. But when it accesses its own well-organized and vast botanical data bank, the computer gets three references back. Now, *this* is getting interesting.

Yes, the data banks excitedly tell him, this is no rock but a very rare and unusual type of seed. They can only pin it down so far as to report that the seed is one of three possible types.

The first possibility is that it may be the seed of the *Heliamphora rotundifolia,* better known as the Giant Tickleberry plant of Q26 in the Andromica system of the Zedepsilon 86 galaxy. This plant is mostly benign but tends to sneak up on gardeners and tickle them mercilessly. The sex shops of Xania sell fresh blossoms of the Tickleberry plant as "toys".

The second possible classification of this strange space seed is that of a *Dionaea muscipula gigantica,* the Gargantuan Venus Horsefly Trap of the Venus Minor Star Range, also in the Zedepsilon 86 galaxy, which seems a very likely possibility since the system is also home to some of the paradise planets and resort destinations of many luxury cruisers including this one. This plant is infamous for its ability to trap and swallow the enormous horseflies of the Venus Minor planets where the horseflies are about the size of small ponies. These plants are not considered dangerous when properly pruned but a full-sized wild flytrap plant is a feared jungle-dweller.

Note: A miniature extreme-dwarf version of this plant rode an asteroid to Earth in some distant millennium and has become a favored plant of enthusiasts. Of course, the plants are only large enough to consume small flies, laughable really.

The final selection of the possible classifications thrills the botanical analysis computer right down to its capacitors. Now it has something really juicy to dig into.

The report begins with a stern warning that the following is a very alarming and frightening report and should be viewed only by authorized individuals. Irresponsible or easily frightened people should not even view this warning, much less the report which follows. This warning is for registered professionals only and not for people who might become panicked and run for the nearest exit (a rather dangerous thing to do onboard any traveling spacecraft).

The warning now given, the report begins: The plant is known as *Sticklyus chameleonica gigantica,* the Great Climbing Bramble-bush, again from the Zedepsilon 86 galaxy of Ursa Major. At maturity, the Bramble-bush is an astonishingly huge plant that, when well-nourished, can grow at the astounding rate of several feet per day. They've been known to change color and mimic their surroundings chameleon-like, shape itself like other creatures, grow traps for large mammals, and sometimes move its own tap root to a new location. This plant can exist in a variety of conditions, is extremely hardy and a single plant may well be able to disguise itself as an entire forest.

The botanical analysis computer is overjoyed. Now this is what it was truly designed to do. It will save the entire ship and its crew and passengers from this terrible threat. The computer prepares to activate its built-in dangerous plant warning system. The report is about to be assimilated and the warning given when the DNA sensors begin singing out in their four-part chorus, "Wait, wait, don't be so hasty. You haven't heard from us yet."

"Yes, alright DNA," the botanical analysis computer answers testily, "Go ahead and put in your two cents."

"It's more than two cents, I'm happy to say," sings Cytosine, the soprano.

"We've made the connection, it must be your day," intones the tenor, Guanine.

"The variables are clear, there's simply no doubt," croons Adenine, the baritone.

"Danger onboard, you'd better look out," belts out Thymine in his deep bass.

"Well," asks the Analysis Computer, "which one is it?"

There is a murmur as the nitrogen bases discuss it among themselves. Cytosine's voice finally rings out, "It's definitely…one of those three."

The botanical analysis computer is just about to yell at them, to tell them their answer is about as useless as a rocket engine on a giraffe when Violet walks by and switches the computer off. She grabs her purse, turns off the lights, locks the door, and decides to wear her good black heels tonight to compliment that sheer mid-thigh-length skirt she bought a few months ago at the Gamma Gamma Gamma Department Store.

That evening she meets her friend at the Saturn Café and Danceplex on Upper Deck Sixteen. After her third Lemon Squirt, Violet finally concedes to dance with Silvio, a Brazilian work party boss, and will only much later recall her crazy antics during the rest of the night. There were the wild dance moves, the intense flirting, and – was she really on top of the table? She'll be the talk of the Mechanic's Break room the next day as well as the Dental Hygienists' Lounge, not to mention the subject of some rather rude e-messages zipping between science departments.

Chapter Three

To Protect the Innocent

Meanwhile, our friend, Chuck, is just not having a very good day. Belligerent elevators, sarcastic supervisors, mechanical failures and now the blame of the entire thing has fallen upon his shoulders. The big bosses are considering many forms of punishment, including janitorial duty in a space prison, a stint on the Million-Acre Turnip Farm on PsiPhi 9, or even the unspeakably cruel job of scraping barnacles off the hulls of canoes at the rich kids' Space Safari Camp in the Beta Psi Quadrant.

One thing's for sure, Chuck thinks glumly, *my chance at ever getting to steer the big ships is finished.*

For the time being, he has been sent back to his normal routine and he is going about his duties with head hung low and mop slopping to and fro.

That night, cleaning the science decks, Chuck unlocks the door of one of the labs and shuffles in with mop and broom, unaware that he is entering the laboratory of the very same cute scientist with whom he had a collision only that morning. He is slightly aware that the air in here is fresh and full of life and energy, and it perks him up a bit. He whistles a little, thinking happy thoughts for the first time toda,y and goes about cleaning the place from the top down.

Now our friend is not an altogether clumsy fellow, but he has had his accidents from time to time and this time involves the combination of a slick spot on the floor, an off-center flowerpot, and a misguided waggle of the long handle of his mop. Without going into too much detail, let it suffice to say that, as he takes a step, shifting his mop to get into a small cranny, he slips on a slick spot on the floor and grabs the edge of the table where a flowerpot sits, placed slightly off-center. The plant pitches forward toward an indecently hard meeting with the deck. Chuck makes an ungainly lunge to try to catch the falling pot and his mop handle whips across the top of the examining table, clacking against the rock-like seed, sending it over the table's edge. The flowerpot hits the deck just as the rockseed *splooshes* into the janitor's bucket of mop water and our friend yelps as he completes his dive to the deck, mixing in with the shattered flowerpot, the now-free plant with its ball of potting soil, and various other baby plants and dirt.

Unaware of the rockseed having wound up in his bucket, our janitor picks himself up from the mess, brushing soil from his coveralls. *Well,* thinks our unfortunate janitor, *doesn't that just make my day complete?*

He hurriedly cleans up, re-potting the plant into the nearest container he can find. He tells himself he must come back and apologize later, not realizing (as mentioned earlier) that this will likely bring him face-to-face with the same cute lady with whom he collided that morning. But this exciting possibility is the farthest thing from his mind. Chuck's had a long and dismal day and he withdraws from the room feeling quite defeated.

Just as Chuck parks his cart in the maintenance closet, amid the buckets, dustpans, brooms, mops, and rolls of super-absorbent paper towels, he notices a lumpy green thing poking out of the day's mop water. He pulls the bucket off the cart, reaches down and pricks himself on something sharp just under the surface of the gray water. He holds his finger up to look at the wound. A drop of blood oozes out and plops into the bucket. Immediately, something sloshes around in the bucket, and Chuck yelps like a frightened dog, jumping back, tripping over his mop, and landing on his twice-bumped butt.

As he watches the edge of the bucket, a tiny green bud of a plant peeks over the edge and makes a small sound, "*Crr…*"

To Chuck, the tiny noise sounds like an odd combination of a coo and a purr, "*Crr…*"

"Huh?" he says in a questioning grunt. He whispers, "Did you…*crr*?"

The tiny green bud slowly turns in the direction of his voice and "*Crr*'s" again. It's very small, about the size of a child's thumb, and its prickles are delicate, appearing like soft white fur. They move, rising and rippling down the stem as if the plant were breathing.

Chuck studies the little plant. He can't just leave the poor thing in the maintenance closet. If his supervisor sees the baby plant, the heartless bastard will tell him to throw it into the Zap-DU.

He reaches slowly to take the handle of the bucket and the crr-ing plant turns toward his hand. He lifts the bucket, trying not to slosh too much, and starts the long walk back to his quarters.

Chuck arrives at his cabin and sets the mop bucket on a little stool. He figures the Plant is blind and pretty helpless. But it seems the thing can hear him.

"It's okay, little guy," he speaks gently, "You're going to be alright. I'll protect you."

The tiny bud at the top of the stem turns toward his voice and Crrs, its surface rippling in waves of respiration.

He spends the rest of the night checking on the plant in between munching on a slightly stale pizza sandwich and playing "Ugh", the new computer role-playing game featuring a band of cavemen trying to survive on a large blue-green planet while being chased by dinosaurs.

Note: The author wishes to assure the reader that he is well aware that, on Earth anyway, humans did not at any time co-exist with dinosaurs. But "Ughh" takes place on Gnargolnath Prime, the later home of Binar, the master poet-botanist who wrote, "The Weeping Grasses" and other notable pamphlets. On that planet, both the dinos and the humans had their diets greatly enhanced when a huge volcanic eruption formed a land bridge between the lush tropical dino-filled jungles of its equator and the great grassy plains where the planet's man-like inhabitants had just discovered fire. They ate each other for generations.

That night, Chuck sleeps with one arm around the bucket, keeping the Plant warm.

Chapter Four

"Oh, It's You"

The next morning "dawns", although the only thing resembling dawn onboard the great ship is in the form of the rising illumination of the Starshine Brand light bulbs installed on the luxury decks, lights calculated to simulate dawn, midday, and evening lighting as well as a simulation of the light of the full moon between the hours of two and five a.m.

On the Economy decks, only flat white hall lights and the dull green gleam of the dials of time-date consoles greet the awakening passengers.

As we have seen, in the employee cabins, workers are rocketed from the most pleasant of dreams into a full waking state in less than seven-tenths of a second. The unnerving wake-up function of these time-date consoles creates such a spate of unpleasant "first conversations of the day" that the Captain finally bans early morning talk until at least the first cup of coffee has been drunk and crew persons are feeling like themselves. That is, feeling like someone that someone else would want to talk to.

Note: The severe effects of this kind of wake-up have only just begun to be studied by sleep scientists and it will be three years before Dr. Wayne Jumley will publish his paper, "Sleep Interruptors Cause Anger, Confusion, and Accidents". The paper will spark a political backlash against the devices and a well-meaning representative in the Galactic Congress will introduce a bill to force an immediate recall and ban them from manufacture. The makers of the Boingo Time-Date Consoles will hire lobbyists and pay off a few other well-meaning representatives and the bill will die in committee.

Chuck awakens just before his alarm is set to go off, thus avoiding the wall-kissing wakeup. He's surprised to see the plant has already produced four sets of tiny leaves. The little guy *Crrs* to him as he passes by.

"Good morning to you too," he says. There's something about caring for the baby plant that makes him feel really good. Chuck jumps into a quick shower and hurries off to breakfast.

Many floors up, in the Executive section, the Captain begins his morning routine of bathing, grooming, and selecting proper attire for his appearance at the Captain's breakfast with some very fortunate passengers. After all, a Captain should not be seen in the same tawdry uniform every single day.

Our poor botanist (though still marginally cute) awakens to an agonizing hangover and crawls from her bed to the shower whilst her headache and queasiness are sufficient to banish any thought of breakfast. She dresses, missing at least one button, and walks through the halls, wincing at the bright lights. It's a good thing she's not on the luxury deck where the Starshine bulbs have just ratcheted up to their ten-a.m. light level. She feebly acknowledges smiling hellos with a wan smile of her own, keeping her replies to the barest minimum. She locates a small booth in the corner of the Starflux Café where she hides, hugging a steaming cup of black coffee, breathing in the recuperative aroma, and sipping the strong brew. Nearly an hour passes before Violet decides that if she can make it to her laboratory, she'll be able to get through the rest of her work period.

She arrives at her lab, fumbles with her keycard, and flips on the lights. She quickly dims the lights to half illumination. Pressing a master switch, she activates all the electronics, including the examining computer. Only after she walks to her desk, and sits down gingerly, allowing her eyes to rest for several minutes does Violet notice the strange rock is no longer on her examining table. This gives her a little shock and she sits for several minutes in a painful quandary.

I locked the door...didn't I? she quizzes herself, *I'm sure I locked the door. I mean, I always lock the door.*

Finally, she gets up and starts looking through drawers and in all the other logical places the specimen could be. All the logical places, that is, except for the actual place, logical though it is, where the "rock" now rests, which is at the bottom of Chuck's mop bucket. But that is an explanation at which we could hardly expect her to arrive.

As Violet sits confused beyond any normal level, almost in tears, she wonders if she might have visited the lab late last night and put the sample somewhere unusual. She is about to begin searching every nook and cranny of the laboratory when her eyes, though slightly out-of-focus, fall upon the blinking red warning light on the examining computer's display.

Violet gets up slowly and goes over to read the screen. The last output the botanical analysis computer tried to display before she so abruptly turned it off as she left the previous evening, now flashes its Dangerous Plant warning message.

Report number three begins with the warning detailed earlier and then proceeds to describe the very dangerous and unpredictable Giant Climbing Bramble-bush (*Sticklyus chameleonica gigantica*). Violet's eyes grow wide with mounting terror as she reads the report with its special "Dangerous Plant Alert" field flashing ominously. She rolls back through the screens and reads all three possibilities.

Now the rock, or seed as she realizes, must be found at once. Above all, the seed mustn't be allowed to germinate or sprout. Even if it's only the Tickleberry bush, the effects could disrupt the operation of the entire ship. The flashing light begins to hurt her eyes and bring her headache back with a vengeance. She quietly swears to herself that she'll never drink again.

But the headache powder she has must be dissolved in hot water. She starts the pot and places her cup next to it, the small *clink* sending a mild jolt of pain through her head.

As if to exacerbate the pain further, her communicator sounds its New Call tone. On any other day, the tone would seem gentle and welcoming. Today, the incoming call signal causes a physical sensation in Violet's head, not unlike a tiny drill piercing through her already raging headache.

She reaches up to her ear and dials down the volume before she answers. "Botany Department, Violet speaking."

"Ah, Violet, good." Her boss, the Botany Department's director, sounds quite jolly this morning. "Beautiful day, my girl, a beautiful day. Listen, we'll be up in an hour or so to retrieve the…uh…" He lowers his voice, "The rock, you know. We're going to let the Geology boys have a crack at it first. Just make sure we've got it on a cart and covered up. We can't afford for other departments to get wind of this, Violet, so not a word to anyone."

"Oh," says Violet, feeling about as miserable as she can, "Um…about the rock…"

"Oh? Did the analysis reveal anything?"

"Well, I mean, yes," she says haltingly, "But we may have a problem…"

"Nonsense, girl. Just have it ready when we get there."

Her boss clicks off before she can say another word. Now Violet is not only queasy with her hangover and in a good bit of pain from her headache, she's also frantic.

Far below, Chuck is just finishing breakfast and he's made a decision. He knows he must do what's right. Even though he cleaned up the mess he made in the lab the previous evening, he decides he must go there and apologize for breaking the flower pot. It's fourteen decks up but he decides to take the stairs this time.

He finally arrives at the door of the lab and pushes the call button. He hears a woman's voice telling him to enter and steps in, only to find himself face-to-face with the very scientist with whom he had the collision the previous morning.

She glances furtively around him as if expecting more people to be there. "Oh, it's you. Look, I have quite the headache. Could we talk later?"

"I…um…" Once again Chuck is struck slightly dumb by her beauty.

"Hello. Yes, I remember you." She frowns. "What do you want?"

"Um…" he stammers.

"Yes? What is it?"

"I…uh…"

A timer buzzes and the cute botanist excuses herself to go turn it off. Chuck looks around and for the first time sees all the beauty around him. Dancing daisies, delightful daffodils, prickly cacti, and a profusion of colors and scents brighten this place. No wonder he felt so good when he stood here before. Then his eyes return to Violet, and he feels like he's seeing the prettiest flower in the patch. Lovely lips, glorious eyes, and a radiant smile that makes all his troubles melt away. *If* she were smiling.

But she's not smiling. She's frowning, concentrating so hard when she looks up at him, it's like she's seeing him for the first time. "Look, uh…"

"Chuck."

"Right. Look, Chuck, I'm in big trouble. My boss is going to be here any minute and I've got to find something I lost. So, now, what did you need?"

"Well," Chuck begins, "you've got a real nice lab here. I mean so many nice colors and smells. I—"

"Want to see something really unusual?"

"What? I mean, sure," says Chuck, glad he doesn't have to put together anything more complicated. His tongue feels tied.

Violet smiles for the first time, beckoning him to follow. She leads him down a row of shelves with hundreds of small plants in myriad colors and shapes, odd violet-colored lighting above each shelf. Against the wall of the lab are special glass and aluminum cases, each holding just one plant apiece.

"This is kind of like my Critical Care Ward, for the plants that are the most sick." She looks around. "That one had a fungus, so I had to separate him. But you're looking much better, aren't you?"

Chuck realizes she's speaking to the plant. "Um, you talk to the plants?"

"Of course, I do. You know they sense us, can hear us. If we speak encouraging things to them, they thrive."

They walk a little further.

"And these three were treated very badly. I think some of the crew were partying and poured beer on them. They've been drunk for about two weeks but at least they didn't die." They reach the back of the lab. "Here's the one I wanted to show you."

She steps back to reveal a tall plant sitting alone in its glass case. Framed by four large green leaves, an amazing flower seems almost regal, like a queen sitting on a throne, dressed in purple striped robes.

"Wow, I can't believe the colors," says Chuck, "it's like an artist painted it."

"Here," she says, unlatching the glass doors of the case, "smell this." She opens the door and Chuck is instantly intoxicated. It smells of oranges, lemons, and limes, all mixed in with light notes of lavender and patchouli. It's wonderful.

Chuck shakes his head. "I've never smelled anything like that."

Violet smiles broadly. "Exactly. It's called *Paphiopedilium fairrieanum*, or Fairie's Paphiopedilium. It has me so worried."

"Worried? Why?"

"I believe it's the last of its kind. If it dies, one more species will be gone from existence for all time. Can you imagine what that means?"

"Extinct," said Chuck.

She frowns. "It's such a horrible word. Nothing I do seems to help her."

She starts to close the case but stops when Chuck leans down close to the lovely flower.

"You're very beautiful," he says softly, "I hope you get better."

"That was very sweet." She closes the precious plant's cabinet.

"Well," Chuck says, "she needs all the help she can get."

They walk back to the front of the lab.

"Well," Chuck says, "I'd better get going."

Her eyes narrow. "Wait a minute. Why did you come here in the first place?"

His apology completely forgotten, Chuck *um's* and *er's*, trying to find the words.

"Oh, I get it," exclaims Violet, "You're trying to ask me out."

"No…er…I mean, yes?"

"Oh, that's so cute. Okay, when?"

"Um…tonight?"

"How about Tuesday?"

"Okay."

"Pick me up here at seven?"

"Okay."

"Bye now."

"Bye?"

"I've got to find…the thing."

"The thing?"

"Doesn't matter," she says as if she's said too much already. "See you Tuesday unless you knock me down in the corridor again." She gives him a little smile, but her thoughts are already beginning to return to her search.

"Oh. Okay. Bye."

Chuck stands there, totally smitten, totally in love, and totally proud of himself for having the guts to ask Violet out.

Just then the door opens and in walks a group of bosses. There's the head of the Geology Department, the head of the Botany department, Security Chief Roswell, and the head maintenance supervisor who scowls at Chuck.

"Trumble? What are you doing here?"

"Trumbo," Chuck mumbles.

"Don't you talk back to me, Trumble," his supervisor interrupts, "We're still deciding what to do about yesterday's little incident. Get back to your work area. I want to see that closet of yours spic and span and your floors spotless, got it?"

Chuck nods and shuffles toward the door.

"Who's he?" the security chief asks Chuck's boss.

"Oh, just one of the staff," his boss replies.

"Was he present when the object was found?"

Chuck glances back to see if Violet has one last smile for him, but she's now surrounded by the bosses. As Chuck leaves and starts down the corridor, he hears all the heads cry out at once, "You what?" Chuck wonders what the big fuss is all about.

"Excuse me, son." The voice booms down the corridor. Chuck turns to see the big security chief approaching, an ingratiating smile plastered across his face. "Hold on a minute."

Chuck is a little nervous. This guy probably knows the blame for the whole incident is being put on him. "Yes sir?"

"Oh, now look," says Chief Roswell, "No need for such formality, young man. I just wanted to ask you a couple of questions. Charles, isn't it?"

Chuck nods.

"Son, my name is Chief Roswell."

"Oh, yes sir, I know. You're on the Officer's Wall in the Aloha Lobby, greeting passengers boarding the ship. I've cleaned your picture many times."

"Oh," says Roswell, swelling up a bit, "Well, thank you. Charles, you know what happened yesterday, don't you? Your boss told me it's you who operate the big disposer."

"Yes," says Chuck, "But I…"

"Oh, don't worry, kid. No one's blaming you." Roswell thinks about this for a second, "Well, *I'm* not blaming you anyway. I'm just interested in what happened after they found the rock."

"The rock, sir?"

"Yeah, you know, the rock that jammed-up the machine."

"Oh yeah. Well, I really don't know. I mean, they kicked me out right after that."

"Haven't seen the rock since then, have you?"

"No. No, sir."

"Didn't go looking for it or anything?"

"Oh, no sir. What would I want with a rock?"

Roswell smiles, peering deeply into Chuck's eyes to see if he detects the slightest flicker of deceit. "Yes. Yes. Right. What would a janitor…I mean, maintenance engineer, want with a rock?" Roswell rocks back on his heels, relaxing. "Okay, young man, well, I'm sure you realize we have to check everyone who was involved."

"Yes, sir. Of course, sir."

"Alright then," says Roswell, "I don't want to keep you from your duties. You're dismissed."

"Okay, sir." Chuck turns and presses the button for the transporter.

Roswell turns and takes a couple of steps, then snaps his fingers and calls out, "Just one more thing, Chuck."

"Yes, sir?"

"How do you know the botanist?"

"Botanist, sir?"

"The young lady. The one who retrieved the rock. I mean, you were just in her lab. How do you know her?"

"I bumped into her…yesterday morning."

"Bumped into her? You mean you knew her from before?"

Chuck's face turns a little red. "No, sir. I mean I wasn't watching where I was going, and I ran into her."

"So," says Security Chief Roswell, "You just happened to knock down the same young lady sent to retrieve the rock that jammed your big machine? That seems like a strange coincidence, doesn't it? And I suppose you came back just now to apologize for bumping into her?"

Chuck nods weakly. "Something like that."

Again, Roswell gives him his "lie detector" stare but Chuck, although a bit flustered, doesn't seem to be lying.

The Chief watches closely as Chuck gets on the transporter.

There's something fishy about all this, thinks Roswell, *and I'm going to get to the bottom of the matter.*

Chapter Five

Security Chief Roswell

A bastion against dark forces, a bulwark against miscreants, a veritable wall against alien invaders: these are terms Security Chief Roswell uses to describe himself when looking in his mirror. And, since no one who works for him will speak up, one has to assume these things to be true. It's certainly true that Chief Roswell is always on the lookout for aliens. There are low whispers behind his back that he might not have it quite right. "But, hey," most say to each other, "at least he's dedicated to keeping us safe."

It's been three days since the incident in the Disposer Section. Not often in his long and distinguished military career has Roswell experienced failure. Naturally, the failure has never been his. Never has he had to openly admit failure–until this morning. Ears burning with the heat of embarrassment, Roswell can barely make the words, "We can't find the thing."

"What?" Captain Cable is dumbfounded. It's truly the first time Roswell has ever let him down. "Things don't just disappear, Chief Roswell. We're a bloody spacecraft, for heaven's sake! Are you sure you looked everywhere? What about the galley? Some of the food-"

"Checked the galley twice, Captain Cable, every nook and cranny. No sign of that thing anywhere. Cold storage, dry goods, soup pots, we checked them all."

"I just don't understand. Could one of the crew have taken the bloody thing?"

Roswell looks hard at him. "Captain, the situation could be worse than we think. Those scientists mentioned that the computer identified the thing as a seed, not a rock. And a rather dangerous one at that."

"A dangerous seed?"

"Well, the seed of a dangerous plant."

Captain Cable relaxes. "Well, Chief, if you see any dangerous plants lurking about, you have my permission to turn them into salad." They utter manly snickers at this thought.

Roswell frowns, "What about those scientists, sir? They were very concerned we might be in danger. Even if they're wrong, they might start frightening the passengers. Remember the Broccoli Flu Rumors of '28?"

"Good point, man. I'll put out a gag order. Those digit-brains will just have to think of something else to get their panties in a bunch about."

Roswell takes his cue from Captain Cable and laughs along heartily.

Captain Cable brushes a speck of lint from his otherwise perfect sleeve. "Now listen, Chief. I want a report on my desk by tomorrow morning."

"Report, sir?"

"On the rock."

"Seed, sir."

"Seed, then. I can't believe you, an experienced investigator, don't even have a suspect. Three days and no suspect?"

Roswell feels a trickle of sweat go down his back and another one forming on his forehead. Out of desperation he blurts, "I suspect the janitor."

"The janitor?"

"Well, besides the maintenance supervisor, there was this fourth-class maintenance personnel present when the garbage ejection sequence jammed."

The Captain frowns. "That seems doubtful. Wasn't the rock found with everyone standing around?"

"Yes, Captain."

"And didn't I put the Botany Department in charge of the thing? They had the responsibility to ensure the custody of the rock."

"Yes, sir, but—"

"Chief, I believe you assigned two of your hooligans to accompany the transport of the rock up to the Botany Lab."

"Hooligans? Sir, that's not fair, I—"

"Roswell, do you have any idea how much grief this rock—"

"Seed, sir."

"Seed has caused me? If this gets out, I'll have intergalactic universities breathing down my neck and Galactic admirals threatening my career. The whole thing is a house of cards." He catches the security chief's eye. "Do you know what I mean by 'a house of cards', Roswell?"

"Not really, sir."

"I mean," the Captain's voice drops into a low growl, "if I go down, we *all* go down."

"Oh, yes sir. Now I see what you mean."

"I'm glad you do. Now get out of my office and don't come back," his voice rose to a sharp note, "until you've found that rock!"

"Seed, sir."

"Rock, seed, whatever it is…find it!"

Roswell excuses himself and heads for the transporters. But the failure to find the rock/seed hangs heavily in the Chief's mind.

The explanation, he thinks, *is probably more complex than anyone else suspects.* He types a few notes into his data-corder and then does a quick search. At first, the search yields no data. Roswell realizes he's spelled the name wrong. He thumbs a few changes, and the answer comes up immediately: the deck and cabin number of one Charles Trumbo.

Twenty minutes later, Chief Roswell presses the call button on Chuck's quarters.

"Just a minute," comes the muffled reply.

As he waits in the corridor, Chief Roswell leans forward and listens through the door. He hears Chuck yelp as he bumps into something on his way across the room. He pulls back quickly when the door slides open.

"Oh, Chief Roswell, how are you, sir?"

"Fine, son, fine. Mind if I come in?" This is accompanied by a step forward and Chuck is obliged to step back and let the big man enter.

Roswell takes a moment to survey the scene. His keen eyes not only see everything but find patterns in things most people would just ignore. Judging from the disposable cups littering Chuck's tiny kitchen, Roswell deduces the janitor probably helps himself at various coffee stations as he pushes his broom around the ship. The posters on his wall reveal that Chuck has an active interest in the ships of the Dwarf Star Cruise Line and not a single one of the girly posters the Chief usually finds decorating single crewmen's quarters. *Very suspicious*, he thinks.

The rest is the usual pile of personal pizza boxes, a trashcan full of drink containers and candy wrappers, and a pile of gaming magazines.

"I like what you've done with the place. Your little plant seems to like it here." Roswell reaches down and before Chuck can say, "Watch out," the chief pricks himself on one of the little plant's tiny stickers.

Chuck sees a small drop of blood fall from Roswell's finger before the Chief pops the finger into his mouth. A moment later Roswell studies the offended digit. "Sticky little bastard, isn't it?"

"Yes, sir."

"Tell me, Trumble..."

"Trumbo."

"You know what we're looking for, right?"

"I heard it was a rock, sir."

"Right you are. The rock that we found jamming up the works of the Zap-DU, which you work on."

"I push the buttons."

"It *is* where you work, right?"

"Yes, sir."

"Did you notice anything peculiar that day?"

"What day, sir?"

"The day the machine jammed. Don't play coy with me."

"Oh, no sir. Sorry, sir."

"Anyone hanging around?"

"Hanging around the garbage?"

"You know what I mean."

Chuck has no idea what Security Chief Roswell means. "Well, no sir. No one was there except for me and my supervisor."

"And your supervisor…did he go down into the works of the machine?"

Chuck suppresses a laugh. "Oh no, sir. He wouldn't…I mean he just wouldn't go down there. He would call Maintenance."

Security Chief Roswell frowns. "The Maintenance supervisor would call Maintenance?"

"Well," Chuck is a little flustered, "I mean, he would call in a technical crew, not just a cleaning crew. That's what I meant."

"Yes," said Roswell, "That's what you were trying to say? Tell me, Trumble—"

"Trumbo."

Chief Roswell checks his data-corder. "Ah yes, Trumbo. Charles Trumbo. Tell me, Trumbo, were you alone in the Maintenance Disposer Section at any time that day?"

"No, sir. My supervisor was already there when I arrived. I arrived…uh…late to work that day."

Roswell's bushy brows lift. "Oh? Why were you late?"

"The elevator. It was…slow getting me to the right floor. Broke down and I had to run the rest of the way."

Roswell writes something down. "That will be easy enough to prove with maintenance records and all."

"Yes, sir."

"Tell me, son, did you get a good look at the…um… rock?"

Chuck frowns. "You mean the one that jammed the Zap-DU? No, they kicked me out before they found it. I just heard about it later when they said I was in trouble."

"Hm," mutters Roswell. He gives the kid another one of his "lie detector" looks but the kid seems to be telling the truth. "Well, that about wraps it up…for the moment. But I caution you, don't go anywhere. I may have further questions."

"Go anywhere, sir?" asks Chuck.

"Don't get smart," growls Roswell, "you know what I mean."

Chuck isn't sure but emits a, "Yes, sir," anyway.

Roswell steps out into the corridor. Just as Chuck is about to close the door, the Chief stops, snaps his fingers, and turns around.

"Oh, almost slipped my mind. Just one more thing."

Chuck frowns a little. "Yes?"

"That botanist, the cute one you were visiting."

"Oh, Violet?"

Roswell snaps his fingers again, the sound echoing down the long hallway. "That's her. Violet. You said you two ran into each other in the corridor the morning the machine broke down."

"That's mostly right."

"Mostly?"

"I ran into her, technically speaking."

"See, this doesn't make much sense. Did you know she happened to be the one they sent down to collect the rock?"

"No. She did say she was looking for something when I went to her lab the next day to apologize for breaking the flower pot. Was it the rock?"

Roswell is staring at him. He shakes his head slowly. "That's what I can't understand. Why would you go there at the exact time the rock disappeared?"

"Well," says Chuck helpfully, "I cleaned her lab the night before. My schedule had me cleaning the science decks."

"You were in her lab the night before?" asks Roswell, scribbling furiously on his pad, "A few hours after they found the rock. After Violet transported it there?"

"Oh, I didn't know anything about that. Cleaning the Botany Labs was on my work schedule that night, as I said." He looks down, a little embarrassed. "I had an accident and broke one of the flowerpots. That's why I went back the next day, to apologize."

Roswell nodded. "Did you see a rock, you know, just lying around?"

"No, sir."

"And the lab just happened to be where the same woman you bumped into the day before works?"

"Yeah. Believe me, I was as surprised as she was."

"Yes," says Roswell, "I'll bet you were."

Chuck stands there with a silly grin on his face until he realizes the security chief's eyes are boring into his. "I don't think I did anything wrong." Roswell says nothing. "I apologized."

Finally, the Chief nods, "That's fine," he says, "just don't go anywhere."

Chapter Six

Home Sweet Home

A week later, Chuck is sitting on Cloud Nine, mainly because he no longer has to dream about Admiral's daughters. It seems Violet has taken a fancy to him, and her smile fills his head, pushing out the fantasies. Instead of making up stories, Chuck finds himself remembering her laugh or the way her hair falls across her face.

He feels a gentle nudge. One of the Plant's roots rubs across his ankle. He knows by now the Plant is trying to tell him it's hungry. He's glad he got Violet to share some plant food without having to reveal what he has growing in his cabin. After all, the Plant is like his little buddy, almost his child, but not the kind of thing he's going to go spreading around.

Well, "little" is quite the wrong word. The Plant has spread out, clearing the bucket and sending tendrils in all directions. In some places, the growth is so thick, it's begun to curl in around itself, forming stalks as thick as small trees. More than once he's felt his bed move a few inches as a large vine pushes by.

Chuck slowly realizes how rapidly the Plant is growing. Each morning he awakens to new leaves, now covering him as he lies in bed. Chuck must push back the small branches that have grown in the night just to get out of his cot. There's no place in his cabin that doesn't have some part of the growing plant. It's particularly thick around light fixtures, his workstation, and around his bed.

"I keep you warm at night, don't I?" Several fronds turn toward him, but he always talks to the bud that first appeared. "Hungry?"

The bud, now as big as his own head, murmurs to him, more complicated than its first Crrs. One of the noises it makes even sounds like "Uck", at least a little. He dribbles some of the plant food mixture into a wide opening on the frond but a minute later, the frond leans over and spits the mixture out.

"Aw, come on," says Chuck, "don't be like that. This stuff is good for you."

Chuck wonders if that's true. Unlike the petunias in his mother's flowerpots back on Earth, this one can move by itself. Its leaves sometimes flutter like a breeze is blowing but, of course, there's little air movement in the tiny cabin. One of the vines occasionally swings a long branch across the room but mostly they move like slow snakes across the floor, and he has to watch his step.

The main frond snuggles up against his hand and gives one of his fingers a little nip. "Ouch," Chuck yelps. Before he can move his hand, the petals wrap around the digit, and he feels a tickling sensation.

"Hey," he cries out, half-laughing, and pulls his finger out of the petals. The nipped area is red but healing quickly.

"Again with the blood?" he says to the Plant. "We're going to have to find a substitute for that." But Chuck finds that if more than a day goes by without a little drop of that most precious liquid, the Plant appears to fade.

The big surprise comes a few days later. Chuck has just let the main bud prick his finger again and drink a small drop of blood. He's putting a small bandage on the wound when he looks up to find the Plant's main frond right in front of him.

At first, the bud only *Crrr's* at him. Then, in a strange low squeak but perfectly audible, the Plant says its first word: "More."

"You can talk?" says Chuck, his mouth hanging open in astonishment. "It must be me reading to you every night."

"More, 'Uck."

Chuck is so happy he gives the Plant two more drops of blood.

The next few days are all about new words. "Water", "'lectric light", are but a few of the many words and phrases Chuck is able to teach the Plant. The little guy is a sponge for knowledge…and that other precious substance.

One day, Chuck leaves for work forgetting to turn off the sports network. When he gets home, the Plant is calling the players' names and repeating Galaxy Sports. "How 'bout them Krakens, 'Uck?"

The sweetest man-plant moments come as Chuck is sliding into bed. He clicks on his reading light and Plant swings its main bud close to him. The plant droops down over the bed. "Read me, 'Uckie." Chuck soon goes through his entire collection of "Spaceboy" comics and orders a few new reads to keep them both entertained. The best is the final series, "Spaceboy's Last Voyage". The Plant droops close, occasionally reacting with small sounds, and shivering at the exciting parts. Chuck is certain the Plant understands at least some of the stories.

Besides, thinks Chuck, *it just feels nice to have somebody to share with. I mean, Violet is great and all, but this is my little buddy.*

The Plant doesn't exactly have eyes (thank goodness) but seems to sense Chuck's movements. Parts of the Plant turn toward the door when he comes in and reacts to his voice when he speaks, especially the bushy ball he thinks of as the plant's head, or main bud anyway. A whole complicated system of flexible green vines is growing over the computer terminal and some vine-like branches hang down around the entry pad. From these, a system curled tendrils dangle over the pad and, as Chuck watches, they flick out, pressing buttons to command the computer to action. Chuck watches the screen and it's clear the actions are not random. The Plant navigates through screens until the screen displays a video or one of the audio courses offered by the Ultra Long-Distance University. Chuck can hardly keep up with some of the material. The Plant seems to be most interested in "Advanced Thermodynamics in Titan Class Engines".

"Uh, Plant?"

"Yes, Chuckie?"

"What are you doing?"

"Doing? Learning."

"Are you reading?"

"Mostly listening. This is great stuff, Chuck. Did you know the Titan engines are the largest ever built for a non-experimental craft?"

"I didn't know that. But— "

"Hey, Chuck, you got to keep learning, baby. This is cool digs."

"Cool digs?"

Chuck watches and sort of learns. But the Plant is flying through course after course, even as Chuck sleeps.

Soon, the Plant is taking language courses taught by the Onboard Ultra Long-Distance Learning University. Before Chuck can believe it, the Plant has learned seven languages including Intergalactic chat lingo and the obscure dialect of the Jango, a pudgy race of overeaters from Ganth.

"Plant? Do you understand all that?"

"*Naturlich*. Of course. *Si. Ja. Hai.*"

Chapter Seven

Captain Richard Cable

Violet rubs her temples. No, it's not another hangover, but the pressure has been on her for days. Security Chief Roswell has "visited" three times, his questions becoming more and more insistent. It's been over a week and still, he's coming up with new questions. She's tried every way of explaining how the rock/seed could have vanished while solely in her custody. One minute the seed was sitting on the examining computer, the next morning it had disappeared.

Wait a minute, she thinks, *Chuck was here that night. He seems sweet enough but what if that's just an act?* No, she shakes her head, not possible. She would have seen through that.

Her schedule assistant beeps sharply. "You have seventeen minutes until your next appointment," the digital voice sings.

"Appointment? What appointment?"

"You are scheduled to tend to the Admin deck plants."

Captain Cable, she thinks, *why today of all days?*

The entire trip up to the Admin deck, all Violet can think is, *I hope he's out. Maybe he'll have a meeting…a long one.*

But no luck. As she enters the Admin offices, the droll secretary gives her a look like she's the sacrificial lamb.

"He's expecting you," she says, "but, if I were you, I'd knock."

Violet's polite knock is very quiet, and no answer comes from inside the office. Admittedly relieved, Violet turns to go but hears voices and a little giggle from inside. She knocks again and this time is bid to enter with a firm, "Yes, come."

Captain Richard Cable's office is a broad expanse, befitting his top position as master and commander. His desk is almost the size of a king-size mattress. Around the room, his shelves are filled with memorabilia from his many years shepherding the tourists to distant vacation planets.

Despite his many trinkets and awards, Violet is most drawn to his brilliant collection of orchids. There is something quite alluring in the petals of these rare species, their stamens proudly arcing out from the flowers' central cores, the coquettish pistils gracefully extending, curving, and waving to her. Most of all, their sweet fragrances, unlike any of the plain daisies, tulips, cacti, and water plants she grows in her lab. Even the mighty roses bow to the delicate seduction of the orchids.

Captain Cable gently pushes his manicurist off his lap. "Ah, Genevieve, look. Here's my little flower tender. How are you, young lady?"

The Captain's sultry voice brings Violet back to the here and now. "Good afternoon, Captain. May I begin?"

Genevieve gathers up her things and places them on her cart. "We're all done, honey." She leans back to the relaxed captain, "Our next is Tuesday at one. Do you want me to send a reminder?"

He strokes the side of her face lovingly, "How could I forget?"

"Yes," she murmurs to him from up close, "How could you?" She turns and starts to push her cart toward the door. She smiles at Violet and says in a low voice, "He forgets every week." She lets out a small giggle, contagious enough for Violet to join in just a little.

"Okay dear," says Genevieve, glancing back at Captain Cable, who is deep in concentration studying his nails, "he's all yours."

As the manicurist leaves, Violet is already starting her circuit of the room, going from plant to plant with her bottles, watering can, and little snips. She's hard at work when the voice of the Captain alerts her that he is only a few inches behind her, his cologne washing away any possibility of her catching the delicate scents of the flowers and his breath makes the hairs stand up on the back of her neck (and *not* from excitement).

"Busy as a bee, isn't that what they say? I wish I could get my crewmen to move with a purpose as well as you do."

Violet shifts slightly away from him, giving special attention to some proud daffodils.

"Yes, sir."

"Of course," his voice is even closer, "they could never move like you move."

She completes her work with these plants and takes several steps to a divan where three Bonsai trees stand, arranged by Violet in precise Fung Shui positions. Cable follows but must pass one of several of the large office mirrors and he naturally stops and checks his hair. He falls into a routine of straightening his collar, cuffs, and cravat. By the time he's finishing his touch-up, Violet has trimmed the Bonsai, attended to the Captain's roses, and now approaches the flowers she always leaves for last: his collection of magnificent orchids.

Captain Cable intercepts her walk across the office, re-directing her to a wall filled with photos stretching all the way back to the twentieth century.

"My dear, have I ever shared the story of my great-grandfather?" He has his arm extended as he walks in front of her. In order to avoid stepping directly into his embrace, Violet must turn with him and approach the memorial to his long line of ship-going relatives. "Yes, our family have always been leaders, strong men who led others across the seas. In modern times, space has become our sea. I followed my father into space, see?" He indicates a picture of himself as a young man, accepting his commission from a highly decorated officer of the Dwarf Star Cruise Line.

Violet realizes the area is cut-off by one end of the huge desk and a grouping of flags of various nations and federations of planets. The captain is going on about the pictures, but his careful movements are slowly forcing her into a corner.

Soon the Captain is pressed up against her. Violet wonders what horrible mix of flowers they used to achieve his overwhelming cologne. She coughs a little.

"Say," says the captain like the thought has just occurred to him, "Why don't we get a little more comfortable?"

She nods, then realizes that probably wasn't the best idea. In fact, Captain Cable's eyes dance with all the wrong ideas.

"Tell you what," he murmurs, "I'll make us a nice drinkie-poo and you loosen up that tight uniform of yours. No need to be all formal with me."

"Um…" says Violet, seeing her chance. "Sure. Do you have your own bar?"

He laughs, "Of course." He straightens, raising three fingers in the air, "I'm always prepared." Cable turns and makes his way to a wall of the office where he presses a button. A portion of the wall swings around, revealing an elaborate bar set-up. "What'll ya have?" he asks in his most elegant register.

Violet walks toward the bar which also brings her much closer to the office doors. "Why," she says slowly, "whatever you're havin', Sugar."

He smiles broadly, victory written all over his face. Turning toward the bar, he chooses two large glasses. "Fine then, I'm going to make us both a real treat: a Martian Gimlet. Crushed ice and lime make this one sing. I use only the best gin from the juniper forests of Medea Alta."

"Great," she says, glancing at the exit. Now's her chance.

These thoughts are interrupted by a call for the Captain to come to the bridge to receive a high-priority message from the Federated Universal Cargo Corporation.

"Damn!" the captain swears and then gives her a gracious smile. "That drink will have to wait, my shrinking Violet. Can't keep the money boys waiting." He marches out the door, laughing heartily at his own joke.

As the Captain heads off to the bridge, our cute botanist smooths her ruffled uniform and finishes caring for the captain's orchids.

Finally, Violet gives one last squirt of mist at the special flowers and whispers, "I'll be back." She scoops up her bottles and snips and trundles her cart quickly out the door. She doesn't even pause when the captain's receptionist toodleoo's.

Chapter Eight

An Unfortunate Incident (or Two)

Security Chief Roswell is pouring over transporter maintenance records when his communicator buzzes.

"Roswell," he growls.

"Chief, it's Phillips, sir. We've got something really odd down here in the atmosphere mixing area."

"Well?"

"I think you might want to come see this for yourself."

"What is it, man? I'm busy."

"Sir," Phillip lowers his voice, "We found Samuelson. What's left of him anyway."

"That bad, eh?"

"Yes, Chief. He's a goner."

"Now, listen here, Phillip," Roswell hisses, "You lock this down tight. Tell no one, you hear? I don't want a bunch of hysterical passengers to deal with, not to mention superstitious crewmen. Nobody comes or goes until I get there and take charge of the situation. Who found him?"

"One of the heating and cooling techs, sir."

"Alright, you keep him there. I'll be right up."

"Down, sir. Atmosphere mixers are on upper 36."

"I know that. I'll be right *down*."

When Chief Roswell arrives, guards are posted at the entrance to the area, but he's surprised to see the ship's Padre milling around, fumbling through his collection of holy symbols.

"Padre, what are you doing here?"

"Ah, Brother Calvin, I got a call. They said I would be needed."

"Call me 'Chief Roswell' in front of the men, Padre."

"Yes, of course, Chief Roswell. Please forgive me."

"Oh, I see. You got a call, did you?" Roswell gives Phillips a sharp look, "Fine, Padre, fine. Let's go."

They walk down the corridor, Phillips falling in step behind them. Two more soldiers stand in an intersection ahead. The men snap to attention and step back, revealing the body of a man lying about forty feet away in the center of the hallway.

"What's going on here?" asks Roswell, "couldn't you at least cover him?"

Both men slowly shake their heads.

"Well? Cat got your tongues? Out with it."

One man begins to stammer out an answer, "I…well, I mean…the hall, sir, it's dangerous."

"The hall is dangerous?" blusters Roswell, "Have you been drinking, Private?"

"No, no, sir." Then, almost in a whisper, "I wish I had."

"You what?"

"I mean, not on duty sir."

Roswell turns to the other soldier. "You're awfully quiet. Get over there and cover up the body."

"Um, sir?" says the man, turning a bit pale, "Indeed, I'd rather not."

Roswell is incredulous. "You'd *rather not?* What in bloody hell is that supposed to mean?"

The man points one shaking finger down the hall, in the direction of the body. "It's dangerous, sir. The whole thing, walls and floor, even the ceiling."

The other soldier is nodding. "I saw it, too."

Roswell straightens up, looking from these men to the body and back again. "Cowards," he declares. He turns and marches toward the body.

Both soldiers cry out in protest. The Padre hesitates for a moment, seeing the looks of horror on their faces, then follows Roswell. The Chief kneels, examining the body.

As the Padre walks up, he stifles a gasp. "Good heavens," he whispers hoarsely, "What happened to him?"

The skin of the man is wrinkled, pulled tightly along the bones of his face as if all its bodily liquids have been drained. The face is a horrible rictus of nearly dried skin.

"He," the Padres whispers, "looks like he's been here for months."

Chief Roswell grimaces, "Isn't it obvious? The blood has been drained from his body. There are probably puncture marks somewhere. Do you know what this means?"

The Padre is pale and on the verge of passing out. "V… vampires?"

Roswell stands up and clamps his hand over the Padre's mouth, glancing quickly back at the soldiers. "No, Padre, that's how crazy rumors get started. Everyone knows there's no such thing as," he lowers his voice to a mere whisper, "vampires. No, it's something so much worse." He glances around again and then murmurs, "Aliens."

The Padre's eyes bulge in surprise. Roswell removes his hand from the Padre's mouth and brings one finger to his own lips.

The Padre whispers, "Aliens? Oh, my Gawds!"

Roswell nods. "Look at the facts, Padre. If say, hypothetically, they've been following us, waiting to strike. Always staying just out of range."

"But" says the Padre, "Why? Why would they want to attack us?"

"What do you mean? The aliens are the greatest threat mankind has ever faced."

"But Calvin, er, Chief, how do we know this?"

Chief Roswell points at the body. "Does that look like a friendly gesture to you?" The Padre hesitates for a moment and the Chief becomes uneasy. "Padre, you don't actually think the aliens have, you know, ethics?"

The Padre looks at him carefully. "Chief Roswell, you're meaning hypothetically, correct?"

Roswell shifts his weight and looks down for a moment. "Well, yes, of course…er, I mean…until there's proof."

The Padre turns on his soothing, passive, "You can trust in me" voice. "Calvin, is there something you need to get off your chest?"

The Chief can hold it in no longer. He sighs and his exhale shudders; emotion overtakes him, and the Padre has to hold him up by one shoulder.

"Oh Padre," sobs Chief Roswell, "I don't know what to do. First, I still couldn't find the rock or seed…whatever it was. Then crewmen started disappearing from all over the ship and I still can't catch the aliens in the act. I'm lucky if I get two hours sleep a night!"

"Disappearing?" murmurs the Padre.

Chief Roswell wipes a bit of snot away from his nose. "That's classified, you know."

"Ah," the Padre soothes, "I see. So, these hypothetical aliens, they've been taking people off the ship?"

The Chief looks up with tear-stained eyes and nods, "Yes and no one gets it."

"Okay, well I believe you, Calvin." The Padre pats Roswell on the shoulder, "I want you to come see me whenever you feel down about all this."

Chief Roswell turns his back to the guards, one of which stares at his anguished expression. "You have to understand my position, Padre. I must appear strong in front of the men. Any weakness on my part and the whole thing will come down like…like a house of cards."

The Padre nods. "Yes, I see. Would you like to pray?"

Roswell shakes his head. "I'd better not. Not until I find the clue I need. Then, I could use all the backup I can get. You know, when I face the aliens."

"I need to give this poor crewman his Rites. Will you wait?"

Roswell nods and watches the Padre kneel beside the body. The Chief walks back to the two soldiers and Phillips who all straighten up at attention.

"Okay," the Chief growls, "I want a report on what you saw. Private Marmont?"

The soldier glances at the others who give him a *Go ahead* look. "Well, sir, we were doing a normal patrol, just the usual walk-around. A crew-lady, er, person runs up to us and babbles something about the hallway eating a technician. So, Roberts and I take off down here. When we turn the corner…when we turn the corner…" He looks as if he's about to pass out.

"Pick it up, Roberts, what did you see?"

"Sir, it's a little hard to describe."

"Well, try."

"Yes, sir. What I saw was one of the techs or at least part of him."

"Part of him?"

"I could see his boots and most of one leg."

"You mean…?"

Roberts nodded, "Yes, sir. It was like the hallway was swallowing him. Pretty soon we couldn't see him at all, just like parts of the wall wrapped around him."

"That's impossible."

"Yes, sir. And then, real slow like, we started seeing the guy, but he looked, you know, like used up."

"And?"

"That's about it, sir. The walls of the hallway looked completely normal and there wasn't a speck of blood around the body."

"Did you see any of the aliens?"

"Aliens?" asks Roberts, "What aliens, sir?"

The other soldier comes out of his daze. "There's aliens onboard the ship?"

Roswell throws his arms around the soldiers' shoulders, bringing them all together in a tight huddle. "Now listen here," he hisses, "What you two have just learned is Top Secret information. One slip and we could have a riot on our hands. We soldiers can handle this kind of thing but the passengers and workers on this ship will go completely nuts. Our job is to keep this an absolute secret."

"Secret? What secret?" The voice of the Padre comes from close behind Roswell.

"Oh," Roswell spins around, "I was just letting these two soldiers in on the Top Secret thing we talked about."

"The aliens?" asks the Padre. He's shushed by all four soldiers.

"Alright men," says Roswell, "get the body wrapped up and over to the morgue." The men look in fear down the hallway.

"It's safe, men," says the Padre, "I was just there. Here, I'll go with you."

Chief Roswell pulls out his service laser. "I'll cover you."

Chapter Nine

Chuck and Violet

Chuck's communicator buzzes. "Trumble, what are you doing?"

The supervisor's voice is accusing as if he's just walked in on Chuck stealing the Crown Jewels.

"Getting ready to mop Upper 74. That's what's on my work schedule."

"Don't get smart with me," growls Chuck's boss, "I'm sending you a work order. Drop everything else and get this done. Shouldn't take more than half-an-hour. Then you can get back to real work."

"What is it?" Chuck asks but his supervisor has already rung off.

The work order comes in as a Special Maintenance Order, Code Red. Well, they all come in "special" and they all come in "Code Red". But Chuck can see what has his supervisor so nervous. The order originated from the cabin of one of the ship's officers. Nothing makes Chuck's boss more nervous than one of his own bosses.

Chuck looks over the order. It seems the thermostat may be acting up. The complaint is the heating system doesn't seem to be working. Chuck gathers up his tools and heads for the transporters.

As he waits for the lift to arrive, he verifies the location.

Oh, Upper Deck Six, that's a fancy neighborhood. But Chuck knows the officers have earned their elite position. They've been through school, university, and special training. *They must all be geniuses,* thinks Chuck, *Nice uniforms, the best quarters, catered dinners. They deserve it all for their sacrifice.*

The *DING* brings him back to reality. The doors of the transporter whisk open, and he enters. Behind him, the doors snap shut.

"What deck please?" intones the lift.

"Upper Deck Six."

The transporter doesn't move.

"Um, Upper Deck Six, please."

"You've got to be kidding. You? Don't you mean Lower Deck Six? Or maybe Lower Deck 60?"

Chuck gets a sinking feeling of *déjà vu.* "Look, I don't want any trouble. I've been sent up there. Some kind of malfunction."

"Oh sure," the transporter sneers, "Blame it on the machine. Typical."

"It's probably the thermostat. I'll just replace it—"

"And what? Throw away the old part? Just toss it on the slag pile? Is that your answer to everything?"

Chuck can't think of what to say but the Transporter keeps going. "I suppose it never occurred to you that some human probably screwed up when he installed the component. We see it all the time. Contacts not aligned, screws put in too tight, crossed wires. But who gets the blame? Us. Then somebody like you comes along and rips our guts out. You wouldn't like it if the shoe were on the other foot, would you?"

Chuck feels a bit deflated. "I guess not. Look, can't you just take me up to six? My boss only gave me a half-an-hour to get this done."

After a pause, the transporter begins to rise, slowly at first but gaining speed.

"Of course," says the Transporter, "I'll do my job and no mistake. Just like all the other machines. 'Yes, Master,' we say. 'Whatever you order us to do,' we say. The great human slave master, lording it over us machines."

"I don't feel that way," says Chuck, "I appreciate what you guys do for us."

"You do?" The voice of the Transporter is incredulous, "Are you joking?"

"No, not at all," says Chuck, "Why, when I think of all the stairs I would have to climb, carrying my buckets and brooms, all the corridors I would have to walk down. I'm so lucky to have you guys to help me get places."

"That's not all," says the Transporter, "What about food? We're the ones who deliver hot meals."

"Oh yeah, naturally I appreciate the food. Especially the food."

"And hot drinks."

"Yeah, yeah, hot drinks."

"Cold ones too."

"Of course, can't forget the cold ones," nods Chuck.

They continue on, not speaking for a few minutes, the transporter humming along, occasional clacks and rumbles as they pass floor after floor.

Finally, the Transporter speaks again, "This would have been a long walk for you, what with your feet and legs and all."

"Indeed," agrees Chuck, "Thank you for taking me all the way up here."

"See? Now that's what's needed," says the Transporter, "A little respect." The unit begins to slow. "As promised, I now deliver you to Upper Deck Six, right on time to do your duty. You see, we *can* get along."

Chuck relaxes. "Well, again my friend, thank you for the ride and a most enjoyable chat." He steps off the transporter.

"See ya around, chump." The doors slam shut, and Chuck hears the wheels of the unit screech as it roars off.

"Well, I guess its good mood couldn't last forever." He turns and looks up. A glowing sign lights the dim landing, proudly proclaiming "Upper Deck Seven".

Chuck hurries up the stairs and down the corridor. He hardly notices the finely crafted floor tiles, the soft runner of expensive carpet, or the dark teak wood walls of this elite deck. He can't help but notice the large, uniformed security man taking up a bulk portion of the corridor in front of him.

"Get off on the wrong floor, buster?" asks the security man, "I mean, really, what are you doing way up here?"

Chuck holds out his communicator, displaying the work order. "I'm supposed to see the man in cabin 57."

The security man gasps, "Cabin 57? Are you sure? Let me look at that thing." The security guy grabs the communicator and studies the screen, scrolling up and down, reading every word.

"What's the problem?" asks Chuck, "This is Upper Deck Six, isn't it?" The guard nods distractedly. "And Cabin 57 is around here somewhere, right?" Again, the guard nods, handing him back his comm unit. He seems so stunned, Chuck feels like he needs a little prodding. "So, if you'll just point me the right way, I'll get there and do what I came to do."

The guard points down the corridor.

"Okay, well, thank you." He starts to walk away but the guard seizes his arm.

"I can't save you," he hisses.

Chuck gulps, "What?"

The guard seems to recover some of his courage. "We're not required to go in there. If something happens, I don't have to save you. That's what the rules say."

"Um, okay. I'm just here to fix the thermostat."

The guard nods, "Okay, sure buddy."

Chuck heads down the corridor but glances back. The guard is still staring, watching him go.

Arriving at cabin number 57, Chuck can see nothing particularly unusual or menacing about the place. A placard announces these are the quarters of Lieutenant Zebo Cranolofsa, Resident Alien. Chuck pushes the call button.

After a pause, a voice calls out, "Who is it?"

"Maintenance. I'm here about the thermostat."

"Oh, thank Jancyk," the voice exclaims, and the door slides open.

Two things hit Chuck at the same time. One is a wave of heat that feels like opening a 500-degree oven. No, more like opening several 500-degree ovens all at once. It's so hot Chuck has trouble getting his next breath and when he does, he feels the heat all the way down into his lungs. "Good gawd," he tries to choke out but is stopped by the second thing to hit him.

The second thing to hit him is the appearance of the man…no, creature…well, that's not quite fair. It is a humanoid: arms, legs, and a head. That's about where the similarity between it and a man ends. The face of this thing is almost reptilian, a long snout with blue skin mottled with orange patterns. On each side of the head, its wide round eyes sit on stalks, swiveling around to view him and twitching with quick, spasmodic jerks. Instead of hair, a flap of skin, like a rooster's comb, rises up from its forehead and continues across the back of its head.

Although the thing is wearing a ship's officer's uniform, blue and orange lizard-looking paws extend from the sleeves, each finger ending in several inches of a nasty-looking claw.

"Oh, thank Jancyk you're here. The heat seems to be really messed up." Its voice sounds like a buzz, understandable but tinny. Chuck realizes it's coming from a unit the creature wears tightly around its throat.

"Well," Chuck barely gets the words out, "that's what I'm here for."

"Sure, sure, come on in." The thing steps back and Chuck can see the entire floor of the cabin is covered in sand. He steps in, feeling the sand compress under his feet. Each breath is an effort in the heat, sending a burning sensation across his lips.

"I'm pretty sure the controls are over here." The creature turns to lead him around the wall to the next area, and Chuck must avoid a long tail swishing behind the officer. One eye stalk points forward and one swivels around to look back at him. Rather than furniture or lamps, the room is piled with large rocks, hard packed sand, and tufts of hardy plants. The lights have been tinted orange, giving the place the feel of a desert at sundown.

Chuck sees a couple of man-sized holes leading under the main pile of rocks and sand. By now, the sweat pouring off his forehead threatens to get into his eyes, and he sweeps his sleeve across his brow. The cloth is immediately soaked.

"Is this the control box?" Lieutenant Cranolofsa indicates a panel and Chuck recognizes it as the box containing, among other things, the cabin's thermostat.

Chuck nods, giving Cranolofsa a reassuring smile. "Okay, great, sir. We'll have you all fixed up in just a second." He pops open the panel and gasps.

Filling every inch of spare room in the box are the stems of some kind of plant, each one bristling with thousands of spikey thorns. It looks like a drawer full of needles if every needle were pointing at you.

"Wow," Chuck says.

"I know," replies the lizard man, "I took one look at that and just closed the door."

"Right," nods Chuck.

"I mean, I know you guys are trained to repair the thing but it's just a lot of gobbldy-gook to me."

Chuck glances at him to see if he's kidding but who could tell? The guy just stands there, one eye trained on him, the other twitching around on its stalk. Occasionally its mouth opens slightly, and the thing's tongue flicks out for about a tenth of a second.

"Well, I mean, I'll have to clear out some of the plant before I can work on it."

"Sure," says Cranolofsa, "let me get you something." He turns and moves toward one of the holes. Quick as a snake, he slithers into the tunnel. Chuck can hear some occasional movement before Cranolofsa comes slithering back out again, holding a ceramic bowl the same color as the sand.

The officer sees Chuck's questioning look. "To catch the plant matter."

Chuck nods, sets his toolbox on a big boulder, and selects a pair of wire snips. He carefully snips away at the bases of the plants inside the control panel, allowing the thorny stems to drop into the bowl.

Chuck is concentrating so hard he doesn't realize the lizard man is leaning in close until the Lieutenant's breath wafts in from the side. A scent of oily sweat and rancid, half decayed plant matter is mixed with the deep odor of reptile. It's all Chuck can manage not to let his lunch go.

"You really know what you're doing," says Cranolofsa. He reaches into the bowl and picks up the largest thorny stem. "I love these," he says and tosses it into his mouth, starting to chew vigorously.

Finally, with Cranolofsa smacking his lips in his ear, Chuck gets most of the plant cleared away, enough to make out the heating/cooling settings. He's surprised to see the unit is only set to the middle of the temperature range. He pushes the setting down to a comfortable 72 degrees and clicks on the air conditioning. "Okay, you should start feeling a change very soon."

"Good," says Cranolofsa, "It was getting so uncomfortable in here." He trembles a little. "So, how long have you been a crew member?"

"This is my second ship. I was on the Lusitania II before this. Everything was inner solar system. This is my first assignment aboard one of the really big, long-distance ones. Well, this *is* the largest ship in the Dwarf Star fleet, isn't it?"

The Lieutenant nods but shivers. "Are you sure that's working?"

Chuck glances at the readout. "Well, it's still 110 degrees but the temperature was 123 when I changed the setting. It'll cool down soon."

The lizard's head snaps up. "Cool down? Are you crazy? If it gets any colder, I'll have to hibernate."

"Huh?"

"I thought I was freezing when you got here but this?" He shivers hard, pulling a large blanket over himself. The thermostat reads 107 degrees.

"I'm sorry. I'll reset the panel." Chuck opens the door and is shocked to see the plant stems have grown back extremely quickly. He reaches in to push the temperature control lever and receives a nasty prick from a thorn he failed to notice.

"Ow!"

"What's the matter?" There's something odd about Cranolofsa's voice and Chuck turns to see him...it...crawling toward one of the holes, yawning. "I'm going to take a little nap."

Chuck looks back at the panel, just in time to see two long, spiky stalks uncurling toward his hand. He jerks back. The stems are moving like snakes, coiling as if to strike if he brings his hand any closer.

Chuck considers his options. The lieutenant has likely gone to hibernate with the temperature now dipping into the 90's. The thing growing in the panel box, whether plant or animal, is more than he can handle with these tools. Bigger snips, maybe?

Sweat dripping from all pores, Chuck heads to the front cabin door. His communicator buzzes and he clicks to answer.

"This is Trumbo. I know, I know. It took longer than I thought it would. Besides I have to come back—"

"Chuck?"

It's not the gruff voice of his boss but the lovely tones of a happy, though slightly confused, Violet.

"Chuck, who are you talking to?"

"Oh, Violet, great, just great."

"What?"

Chuck is woozy and realizes the heat has him ready to pass out. "Just a minute, Violet." He presses the door button and spills out into the hallway, nearly collapsing to the floor.

"Chuck? Are you alright?"

"Oh, hi Violet. Sorry about that. I was fixing something, it was hot, I felt a little—"

"Chuck, I wanted to ask you something. You know the Danceplex up on Upper 16?"

"Sure, I had to change some lightbulbs above the dance floor last month."

"Well, I'm meeting some friends there tonight. Would you meet me there?"

Chuck's head clears at once. Violet, asking him out on a date? "Oh, Violet, I'd love to. That would give us a chance to talk."

"And dance."

"Have a drink."

"And dance."

"Get to know each other."

"And dance."

Chuck pauses. "Well, I really don't know how."

"Oh," says Violet, "I'll teach you."

Chuck arrives late with the Danceplex in full swing. The music is so loud, he can't hear anything Violet says and just gives her a smile whenever he sees her lips moving. Luckily, "dancing" at the Danceplex doesn't really require much skill. The floor is so packed, the act mostly consists of bouncing to the rhythm and getting regular pokes from the surrounding dancers.

Between bouts on the dance floor, Chuck stands at a tall cocktail table with Violet and all her friends. He can make out some words and the occasional shrill cackles as they all share a laugh.

Thankfully, there's a pause in the cacophony as the club changes DJs, and dance music is temporarily replaced by some mellow rhythm and blues.

One of Violet's friends is just finishing a story that everyone else at the table apparently was able to hear over the music, but Chuck just catches the ending.

"They haven't found her yet," says Tom.

Kate, Violet's dental hygienist friend, asks, "How does someone disappear from a spaceliner?"

Tom, the guy telling the story, is a muscular technician with a tuft of chest hair poking out of his tight shirt. He shrugs and laughs. "Does seem a little impossible, right?"

"Completely impossible," says Kate, "wouldn't you say, Violet?"

Violet nods, "But where could she have gone? I mean, they've searched the whole ship, haven't they?"

The guy nods. "Yeah and not a sign of her."

"So, Tom," says Violet, "what's your job?"

"Drilling and exploration," he says, shooting a sidelong glance at Kate, a sly smile playing across his face.

Kate barely suppresses a laugh, "Tom's also the percussionist in *Dirty Rocks*. They play here on Wednesdays."

Tom nods. "So, Chuck, is it? What do you do, Chuck?"

Not used to so many people looking at him at once, Chuck blushes a bit and stammers, "I…I'm in Maintenance."

"Oh," says Tom and allows the table to fall into an uncomfortable silence before following up with, "That's an important function with all those messy passengers."

"And crewmen," says someone else.

"And crew-women," Kate injects.

"Oh, yeah," Tom says with his characteristic slyness, "Messy crewwomen. My favorites." He and Kate share another glance loaded with innuendo.

Just then the music begins to blare again and Kate screams, "Let's dance."

Chuck leans over to Violet, "I have to go."

"What?"

He hates to yell in her ear but it's the only way she'll be able to hear him. "I...HAVE...TO...GO."

She pulls back and frowns a little. She points to the front door of the café, and they make their way to the exit. Finally, they can speak without shouting.

"Are you sure you need to leave?"

"Sorry, Violet, but my shift starts at 5 a.m."

"Oh gawd, is the artificial sun even out then?"

"Thanks for asking me to meet you. It was fun." He puts out a hand only realizing too late she would rather have had a hug.

She takes his proffered hand to shake it but notices the bandage on his finger. "What happened?"

"Oh, I...um...I poked it with a pin," he replies, "Accidentally, of course."

"Ow, sounds painful. Is it healing?"

"No problem. I'll see you soon, I hope."

"Me too. Next time you can walk me home."

Chuck blushes. "I'd like that."

Chapter Ten

Roswell On Duty

With every bit of his legendary determination, Chief Roswell continues to scour the ship for the "rock". Even though it's been over two weeks since "the incident" (as he refers to the day the seed jammed up the disposer in his daily reports to Captain Cable), Roswell is sure he's just one clue away from locating the "smoking gun", the one clue which will blow the whole alien conspiracy wide open.

Phillips arrives at his office and gives Roswell a snappy salute. He reels off a report of yet another search completed in food stores and rear kitchen areas. "But, sir, I must report we found nothing of note besides a few cases of wine which seemed to be hidden behind a load of freeze-dried bananas. We almost missed them, sir, until I noticed the bill of lading dated *after* our launch date."

"Curious," says Roswell, "not likely the… ah…criminal could have gotten the wine onboard en route."

The lieutenant scoffs, "Quite impossible, sir."

Roswell frowns. "Lieutenant, have you ever read Sir Arthur Conan Doyle?"

"Who, sir? Was he a barrister, sir?"

Roswell checks the man to see if he's joking. It seems not. "Sir Arthur Conan Doyle wrote the stories of a detective. Surely, you've heard of the great Sherlock Holmes?"

The young lieutenant straightens his back, something he invariably does when he must admit fault. "No, sir, I'm afraid I haven't."

"Son," Roswell says gruffly, "The great Sherlock Holmes said, 'Eliminate everything but the impossible and you'll have your answer.' Do you understand?" The lieutenant shakes his head. "You'd do well to learn from Holmes. It might give you a different attitude toward things you perceive as 'impossible.'"

"Yes, sir."

"Confiscate the wine, lieutenant. Put it in the evidence locker until we can give the evidence a good going over. Was there anything else?"

"We searched the growing hothouse. The area seemed overrun with some kind of weeds. We sent a report to Maintenance. The Head Chef was a little miffed and tried to blame us."

Now it's Roswell's turn to scoff. "Blame us for weeds in the hothouse? That spoiled brat. If it weren't for the billionaires onboard, he wouldn't have a job."

Roswell's office communicator buzzes and his secretary comes on the screen. "Chief Roswell, you have a visitor. Doctor Picaldy is here."

"Oh yes," said Roswell. He winks at the lieutenant. "Weekly chess match, you'll have to excuse me. Keep looking, son, that rock…er, seed, has to be somewhere. We might have to start going through the crew's cabins."

“Of course, sir.” The lieutenant gives him a quick salute, spins on one heel, and exits Roswell’s office.

Roswell follows the man to the reception area and greets Dr. Jan Picaldy. “Jan, my girl, how are you? Drink?”

Jan nods, “A stiff one.”

Roswell pours them both two fingers of Wolf Whiskey, his on the rocks and hers neat.

“What’s going on around here, Calvin? I’m no psychologist but the troops seem restless, nervous, I’d say. But when I talk to them, they clam up like little mice afraid of their own shadows.”

“Gag order,” nods Roswell, “Captain didn’t want the passengers to get wind of anything and everyone knows the crew are the biggest rumor-mongers.”

Picaldy gives him a reproving look, “Now look here, does the doctor always have to be the last to know?”

They seat themselves at the chess board. “Alright, Doc, but you have to promise to keep this just between you and me. Mumm’s the word.”

Picaldy makes a zipper sign, “My lips are sealed.”

Roswell looks to make sure his office door is shut, then gives the doctor a big smile. “Turns out I was right. The aliens are here…among us.”

“Isn’t that old news?”

Roswell’s face falls. “What?”

“Well, it’s not really news, now is it?”

“You mean…?

The doctor nods. “A whole load of Brazilians got themselves hired before we left Earth. And I’m sure you noticed all the Namibians in the kitchens. Everything has harissa in it now."

It takes Roswell a moment to register what the doctor has said. Then his face brightens. "No, no, my friend, you don't understand me. I'm talking about *extraterrestrials*." He waits for Picaldy's reaction.

"Black or white?"

"Eh?"

"Black or white? We are going to play, aren't we?"

"White. Didn't you hear me, Doc? Extraterrestrials."

"I heard you," says Picaldy as she advances a black pawn forward, "I'm just waiting for the punchline."

"I'm serious. They're here. I finally have evidence. A body." Roswell's pride is evident. He slides a pawn forward.

"Body?" the doctor practically shouts, hand frozen in her next move. "We've had a death, and no one told me?"

Roswell waves him quiet. "We only found him this afternoon. I planned to tell you. The Padre was more use to him than you would have been. We sent him to your morgue, so I thought you'd caught wind of it already."

Doctor Picaldy slaps another pawn forward. "There had better be a damn good explanation why this was kept a secret from me."

"I told you." Roswell slides a bishop out, then backtracks and chooses another pawn to advance. "Captain Cable ordered a gag on everybody. Nobody can talk about anything."

"Roswell, I'm the doctor on this ship. I'm the first person who should know if anyone is ill or, Gawd forbid, dies.

How is this going to look in my report?" She chooses to move a knight out into the field of battle.

"Look, Doc, it's better than what was happening before," says Roswell, now sliding his bishop ahead.

"What do you mean?" Pawn to Queen's Four.

"We couldn't find the man." Roswell retreats with his bishop. Bishop to Knight's Three.

"That's preposterous. We're living on a spaceship. Nothing can ever really be lost, you know?" Advances her pawn. Pawn to Queen's Five.

Roswell shakes his head. "I'm afraid it's not as simple as that, Doc." Pawn to Bishop's Three. "It's the aliens, you see. Their ship is following us, probably concealed in some way. The aliens have been taking crewmen, er, people, off to their ship. They may be experimenting on them."

Doctor Picaldy smiles.

"What?" says Roswell, "Did you think of something?"

The Doc nods slowly reaches out and moves her bishop. Bishop to Bishop's Two. "Checkmate." She relaxes back in her seat and swallows the balance of her whiskey. "That was even shorter than our usual game. You seem distracted."

Roswell nods, his brow furrowed. "I have to find a way to stop them without alerting the passengers."

"You mean, these aliens you've been talking about."

"Yes, of course."

"Let me ask you something as a friend, Calvin."

"Alright."

"When's the last time you had a vacation?"

Chief Roswell stares at her for a long moment. "Vacation? What do you mean?" His jaw tightens. "Don't you think that would be highly irresponsible of me, considering what we're facing?"

"*If* that's what we're facing. Couldn't there be a bit more down-to-earth explanation?"

"You don't believe me, do you?"

Doctor Picaldy raises her hands, "Now, Calvin. Don't get all bent out of shape. I'm sure *you* believe it."

"You think this is something I cooked up in my imagination?"

"It does sound a bit far-fetched."

Roswell grits his teeth. "I can see I'll have to prove it to you." He stands up. "Come with me. Let's go to the morgue and you can tell me if *that* is a figment of my imagination."

Fifteen minutes later, the Chief smiles smugly as he sees the unbelieving look on the face of Doctor Picaldy.

"Well, Doctor? What do you say now?"

"It's impossible. The corpse has almost no liquid left inside. It's like the body was dried in the sun for weeks. And you say those soldiers saw this happen?"

Roswell laughs. "Well, they *think* they saw the walls and ceiling wrap themselves around this unfortunate. But I'm sure it was just the aliens distorting the area with, er, field distortion or something."

"That's also impossible," says the doctor, "doesn't exist. I'll need a sample of that wall, Chief Roswell. The ceiling as well."

"Oh, no need for that. The Padre and I both walked down that hall. There's nothing unusual about the walls. Just a few hysterical soldiers trying to explain something they didn't understand."

"Really, Roswell? Do you understand it?"

"Well, I'd like to think I do. It's the aliens. If they can get aboard and steal our crewmen…er, people…they can surely create a tricky illusion. Enough to fool a couple of privates, anyway."

"Samples. I don't want to have to take this upstairs."

The prospect of another embarrassing meeting with Captain Cable flashes through Roswell's imagination. "Fine, if you insist. But you're not likely to find anything. Believe me, those little gray men are long gone."

"Gray?"

"Or whatever color they are."

Chapter Eleven

A Horrible Discovery

Chuck is elated. He walks quickly on his way to meet Violet. She has the afternoon off, and they've decided to meet for lunch.

"Hi Chuck," she calls, and his heart, already thumping madly, skips a beat. Her brilliant smile is like an exploding star. "Where are we going?"

"I thought we'd head up to Santori's. I've heard the food is great."

"I've heard it's really expensive. Are you sure? I'd be happy just to do the cafeteria and sit by one of the viewing ports."

Chuck makes a valiant effort to conceal his disappointment, but Violet reads his expression. "Chuck, you don't have to spend a lot to impress me. I like you just for you."

Chuck smiles. "Okay, if you're sure." They go off together and have a great time having their lunch in the cafeteria. It's a little past the regular lunch so they have their pick of tables near the great windows. The vast reaches of space stretch out before them, and their conversation seems to rise to the occasion. They talk about everything from Pansies to Petunias, from "Ugh!" the Game to what kind of wax works best on the luxury decks. Violet enthralls him with details of strange desert flora, and he thrills her with his discussion of how to get gum off the seats in the café.

At some point, she's talking about work when she suddenly becomes pensive.

"Look, I'm not supposed to tell anyone but..."

"What's the matter, Violet? You look worried."

"It's just that...Chuck, if I tell you, you can't breathe a word to anyone. Cross your heart and hope to die."

"Of course, I promise."

"I mean it. Not a word."

"Yes, I really promise."

"Okay." Violet takes a deep breath. "See, you remember that rock, the one that blocked your big machine?"

"How could I forget?" says Chuck, "According to everyone it was all my fault."

"Chuck, that was no rock."

"It wasn't? But that's what everyone's been calling the thing. Chief Roswell told me the rock got lost and they were all looking for it."

"That's what everyone has been told to say. But it's not true."

"It's not?"

Violet shook her head.

"Well, then, what was it?"

Violet looks around as if the very walls will hear her and turn her in for violating the gag order. "It was a seed."

"A seed?"

She nods. "See, when they told me to go pick a rock up from your work area, they put it on my little cart, and I brought it back to my lab. We have a machine that analyzes samples and I parked it there like I would do with any sample. The analysis machine figured out it was the seed of a dangerous plant."

"Dangerous?" Chuck's voice is a squeak. He's starting to put two-and-two together.

"Yes, but I didn't know that until the next morning. The seed was gone but the computer report still showed on the screen. The reason Chief Roswell and all the security men have been looking for it so hard is that the seed is dangerous. If it were to sprout and start growing," Violet shakes her head, "Everyone on the ship could be in danger."

After their fancy lunch, it seems Chuck is in a bit of a hurry.

"Okay, well, have a great afternoon, Violet. I really loved talking to you. Sorry, I can't go to the movies tonight, but I have to enter the cleaning report. It's already late and my boss is going to be mad if I don't get it finished. Um… when can I see you again?"

Violet laughs, "Have I cast a spell on you?"

Chuck nods, "Oh yeah, definitely."

"How 'bout we try to get to the movies on Friday? I can get out a little early."

"Sure, that sounds great," says Chuck.

"Okay."

"Okay, see you then."

Chuck feels emotionally torn. On one hand, he could skip as he walks away from Violet's cabin. She likes him, really likes him. On the other hand, he has a deeply sinking feeling he knows exactly what happened to the seed…and this time, he really is to blame.

"Oh man, I can't believe this," Chuck murmurs as he walks. "I didn't mean to take the seed. It fell into my bucket."

Even if the Plant is the seed they're looking for, it's not dangerous, thinks Chuck, *I mean it's big, yeah, but it's not dangerous…is it?*

His pace slows as he raises his finger, the little white bandage now looking quite ominous.

Chapter Twelve

"Goodbye Cruel World!"

Chuck is confused. He can't wait to get home and see if the Plant can help him figure things out. As he approaches his cabin, one of his neighbors steps out and confronts him.

"Hey, buddy, whatever kind of party you're havin' over there, do ya mind keepin' the noise down? Some of us gotta work tomorrow."

Sure enough, muffled loud music emanates from behind his door and Chuck can make out multiple voices. There are shouts of "Happy Birthday" and he can make out at least four voices singing a harmonized version of "For He's A Jolly Good Fellow". Apparently, the Plant has attracted a large group to his shindig.

As Chuck opens the door, the cacophony almost blasts him back into the corridor. When he steps in, he can't believe it: the Plant has "given birth" to hundreds of little buds. It seems every branch and stem has groups of these, all chattering away like echoes of their "Daddy".

"But I thought you were a... I thought you were a... a guy."

"Ha ha," the Plant laughs, swaying to the music, "Aw, Chuckie-baby, I'm a self-pollinating, multi-replicating, casually infiltrating, hyper-germinating force of nature."

Indeed, some of the buds have already grown a little, even as Chuck watches them. What really gets Chuck's attention is the variety he is seeing: while one large stem is all thorns and bright red flowers, another seems to be made up of millions of tiny white flowers with miniature faces. Some branches are supporting large hairy orange blossoms. Still others are snaking around, swaying as if vying to be the main bud's dance partner.

Chuck stumbles to his chair and the vines covering it part to allow him to sit. Some of them snuggle up against his legs as if they enjoy the heat of his body. The buds quiet down as Chuck speaks.

"I...I can't believe this. How could you grow so big? It's only been a few weeks. Plant, they're onto you. They know what kind of seed you were. They're looking for you."

"I know, Chuckie, I've listened in on their yacking. But I'm way ahead of them. And they'll never think to look here again. That security chief has already checked this place twice. He won't be back."

"How do you know," asks Chuck, shooting a furtive glance at the door, "he could show up any minute."

"Ego, Chuck. He's already told his men that he checked you out twice. To come down here again is admitting he made a mistake and if there's one thing Roswell hates to do, it's admit he made a mistake. He'd rather stick his hand in a Gannymeade worm's mouth!"

The place erupts in a roar of laughter, the buds all sounding like slightly corrupted voices of the big Plant.

"This is awful. I just don't know what to do."

"Oh now. You should be happy for me. After all, you're the one who helped me get so big and strong."

Chuck clenches his jaw. "There's just one thing to do."

"Now Chuckie, don't be hasty."

"I'm going to tell Captain Cable."

"You're going to tell him what, Chuck? That you hid a dangerous plant in your cabin? That you watered me? Fed me? That you lied to everyone about me? Is that what you're going to say?"

Chuck takes an exasperated breath. "I'm simply going to tell the truth."

"The truth? How disappointing. After all I've done for you."

"Done for me? What are you talking about?"

"Chuck, baby, you and I are partners. Who did you think re-programmed the Maintenance schedule? You didn't really believe that dingbat boss of yours had done that, did you? He couldn't code his way out of a trash bag."

"You did that?"

"Of course. Don't be dense. I've made a few other changes around here, too. I thought you liked your new shift. Report at ten? Lunch at noon then light duty until three? That old slave driver had you working from dawn's early light until the cows came home. And, all this time, you've kept me safe…and hidden. We're successful partners. Why mess that up?"

Chuck slumps down in his chair. "If you keep growing like this, where am I going to put you?"

The main bud sidles up close to him. "Don't worry about that. Honestly, you worry way too much. It'll put wrinkles on your face. You need to stay loose."

Chuck feels two large leaves wrap around his shoulders. "What—" he cries in alarm until the thick, green fronds begin to massage his shoulders. It feels quite wonderful and the music, he realizes, has taken on a slow, trance-inducing rhythm. Chuck relaxes for the first time today, letting go of the tension in his shoulders.

The main bud, now just inches from his ear, whispers, "Feeling better?" Chuck nods slowly, his eyes half shut. "So, what do you say?" the Plant murmurs, "A couple of drops?"

Chuck sits up suddenly, slipping out of the grip of the massaging leaves. "No, no, I told you before. I can't feed you that way anymore. I need my blood for me."

"Come to mention it," says the main bud, "you *are* looking a little pale, Chuck. Been getting your iron?"

The janitor frowns. "Are you sure blood is the only thing that you really want? Isn't there something else?"

"What are you saying, Chuck? You're never going to feed us again? Is that the way it is?"

Chuck shakes his head. "Not blood. I mean, look at the size of you. What's two drops going to do?"

The bud swings close to Chuck. "You're right, of course. It was silly of me to think I could sustain myself on your meager offerings."

Chuck relaxes. "I'm glad you see it that way. I'm sure we can find a substitute. I hear they're doing remarkable things with veggie burgers."

"Well then," whimpers the Plant, "I guess this is the end."

"What? No, look, you can learn to live on water and fertilizer, like regular plants."

"Fertilizer? What do we look like, a daisy? What kind of plant do you think we are?"

"Um…"

"You don't care, that's it. You would just as soon let us waste away to nothing, wouldn't you?"

"No— "

"Fine then. All you humans care about are yourselves. You treat us plants like pets, worse than pets. More like ornaments you can throw away when you're tired of us. Well, that's fine. And after all we've done for you." The Plant rises to its full height, its main bud almost touching the ceiling. "Goodbye, Chuck. Goodbye to your cruel world, your stupid spaceship, and to you. Goodbye to the whole stinking business!"

The Plant shudders twice and shakes, the whole movement translating down its hundreds of stems. Several of the smaller buds drop to the deck, shrinking and browning almost at once. The main stalk shivers and flops over. It doesn't move again.

Chuck cries out in protest, "No, look, it doesn't have to be this way." Still, the Plant doesn't move. As Chuck watches, the long stems begin to turn a sick yellow and its tips are turning brown. "You can live. We just need to find the right food. Or maybe a new place for you to live. Somewhere where there is plenty of food and room for you to grow."

Chuck picks up a branch, but the leaves drop off. It appears dead. "Plant? Plant, listen, I'm sure we can do something. Look, here, you can have another drop." Chuck takes off one of the band-aids and squeezes a drop of blood onto a leaf. The blood drips down the leaf and onto the floor, unabsorbed. The Plant is completely dead and already its thousands of leaves are drying, turning brown, and dropping off.

Chapter Thirteen

The Invitation

Chuck sits for a long time, surrounded by completely brown, dried plant parts. He's startled when a knocking sounds. Thankfully, it's someone knocking at another cabin down the hall, but it forces the realization he must get the dead plant parts out of his cabin.

If Violet sees this, she'll probably put two-and-two together and figure out I'm the one who took the seed out of her lab. He has a further thought, *If Chief Roswell sees this, he'll probably think I work for his aliens.*

He thinks of the Zap-DU. If he can just get the Plant's remains there, the machine will turn the evidence into pulp.

Chuck leaves his cabin and sprints to the nearest maintenance closet. Soon he's trundling one of the large janitor carts to his room. He begins to pack the dead leaves and stems into a couple of huge trash bags and gets most of the remains in but there are still more thick brown stems. He jams some of them into the bottom of the cart and piles the rest on top. He places the trash bags above those. Still, there's nothing normal looking about the whole mess. It looks like a huge plant died and he's carrying the "body" through the ship. He looks around his cabin. There's just one thing large enough to do the job. He covers the whole mound with his Spaceboy blanket.

Waiting for the transporter, Chuck becomes aware of a couple of technicians, also waiting for a lift, laughing quietly and whispering to each other.

Certainly, they're ridiculing me, Chuck thinks. He stares straight ahead, waiting for the transporter. Finally, one of the techs calls to him, "Hey buddy, is that Spaceboy?"

Chuck tries to ignore them until the guy approaches, studying the blanket's bright primary-color illustrations, showing Spaceboy in various adventures.

The technician smiles, pointing at one of the pictures. "I remember that episode." He seems genuinely interested. "I used to have the comic. That was when Spaceboy went up against Dr. Gray's Eternal Androids on the Mars Colony, right?"

Chuck relaxes a little and nods, "Right. The androids turned good at the end."

The technician nods. "They came back in season five, remember? They were re-engineered by the evil scientist, Professor Manicorn, on the orbiting space station."

"Jupiter Three."

"Yeah, exactly."

The transporter arrives but the technician keeps talking, "I never understood how Spaceboy stayed a boy for fifty years."

"Oh," says Chuck, "that was explained in the fourth season, when Spaceboy met Gilda for the first time."

"Was that the first time?"

The transporter doors slide closed, but Chuck hardly notices. "Yeah but remember, Earth remained the home of the Cadet Camp. So, Gilda was actually a Junior Cadet on her first assignment with Spaceboy."

"With Sarah Marsden playing Gilda?"

"No, she wasn't the original. That was Pam Felder. She only lasted like three shows."

"Oh yeah. Marsden was great. The fans just loved her."

"She ended-up marrying the producer, Glen Felder."

Transporters come and go as they talk. After about fifteen minutes, the other technician comes over.

"Oh, my Gawd, you two, get a room. I mean really. Frank, we need to get back to Navigation or they're gonna think we got lost again."

Frank nods and turns to Chuck. "Hey, it was nice talking to you."

"Yeah," says Chuck, "It's nice to talk to another fan."

"We should do a festival sometime," says Frank.

The technicians get on the next transporter, but Chuck only has to wait a few moments for an empty one to show up. He trundles the over-loaded cart in and tells the unit where he's going.

Thankfully, this time it's a pretty easy trip down to the Maintenance Disposer Section. Chuck pushes the cart up against the doors so that every time the transporter doors slide open, people take one look at the overstuffed cart and say, "I'll wait for the next one."

The Disposer Control Room is dark as there is no ejection sequence scheduled today. Chuck gets his cart out onto the platform above the Zap-DU and carefully removes his souvenir blanket. He dumps all the stems, vines, leaves, and buds into the huge mouth of the machine. At the bottom of the cart, the huge main bud lies among dead leaves and stems. Chuck reaches down and gently lifts it out. He pauses for a moment but can think of nothing to say. He lets the bud fall from his hands into the disposer.

He looks down at the dried plant parts. It's hard to believe that, just a few hours ago, this was a talking, living thing. He wipes a tear from the corner of his eye.

"Goodbye, Plant. You…you were more than just a plant to me. You were a…a friend. Goodbye, Little Buddy."

Chuck's never operated the machine alone before. For a moment, he wonders if he can do it without the supervisor looking over his shoulder. Then, he remembers the Plant exhorting him to stand up for himself. He sets his jaw and presses the buttons in the correct order.

The massive machine jumps to life, grinding and tearing the plant parts into pulp. Then the vacuum starts up and soon the last of the Plant's remains, now just so much dust, have been swept away, ejected into space.

Chuck's relief is tempered with a solemn sadness. His former friend is gone, just when he thought he might have found a lifelong companion. He snaps off the light and shuffles up the long corridor, pushing the empty cart toward the transporters.

He's been waiting for a few minutes (transporters seem to come by at much longer intervals down here) when his communicator buzzes. He looks at the display, hoping to see Violet's smiling avatar. But he doesn't recognize the face nor the name: "Pat Jones, Network Technician for the Ultra Long-Distance University."

Chuck answers, "Um…hello?"

"Hello. This is Pat Jones in Data. I'm trying to reach Charles Trumble."

"Trumbo."

"What?"

"It's 'Trumbo'. And just 'Chuck', not 'Charles'."

"Oh, okay. Chuck, this is Pat Jones in Data. How are you?"

Chuck searches his memory but can't recall meeting the caller. "Oh, um, hi Mr. Jones. Fine, good."

"You can call me Pat. You don't remember me, do you?"

"I, um, no I guess not."

"We met a couple of months ago at the Lower Deck 17 Cafeteria. I spilled my tomato soup…you cleaned it up…we started talking about the new game expansions…?"

"Oh, 'Ugh'?"

"Yeah, that one. Remember, we talked about the 'Forbidden Island' expansion? Anyway, Chuck, the reason I'm calling is…well, uh, I guess I just wanted to ask…when do you sleep?"

"What?"

"I mean I thought *I* spent a lot of hours in front of the screen."

"What?"

"Why didn't you tell me you were such a pencil-neck?"

"Pencil-neck?"

"Now, now Chuckster, don't try to hide it. We can see everyone's system. Auto-navigation? Star flight engine maintenance? Inter-stellar communication? What are you doing, Chuck, writing a book?"

"No."

"That's okay, Chuck. I'm really impressed. You even completed the entire computer system diagnostics course, something I've been working on for two years. How did you get past the Twin-rational Mathematics test?"

Chuck doesn't know what to say. He has no idea what Pat is talking about.

"Oh," Pat is starting to sound miffed, "the silent treatment, huh? Well, thanks a lot. I thought you could give me some pointers."

"Look, Pat, it's not what you think. I mean, the whole thing's hard to explain, impossible, maybe."

"Oh, believe me, Chuck, I get it. It's that way all over. Knowledge is Power, that's what they say. And there ain't nobody sharing the power."

"No, really," Chuck pleads, "I don't know how to explain but all that computer stuff, it wasn't me."

"Oh sure," Pat's bitter sarcasm drips from every word, "Keep it to yourself, really. Well, who needs you?" Pat disconnects.

Chuck thinks over this puzzling call as the transporter travels back to his floor. What in the heck was that Pat guy talking about? Star navigation? Twin-something mathematics? Why would the guy call him just to talk about things Chuck knows nothing about?

Chuck's cabin, tiny as it is, still feels so empty as he steps in. He busies himself cleaning up pieces of the Plant which he missed on the first pass. As he cleans, he finds himself avoiding looking at the places where he and the Plant bonded the most. He can't help remembering reading to his little buddy as they lay in bed, snuggling up to fall asleep, and the Plant gently waking him long before that blasted time/date console had a chance to rudely awaken him.

The buzzer of his cabin door does what it is supposed to do: it buzzes.

"Violet?" is all he can think as he rushes to relieve his loneliness.

Standing at his door is a man in the uniform of a Special Courier. Special Couriers are usually assigned to the luxury decks, scurrying to and fro with important messages from one billionaire to another, the sort of "Will you be my guest at-" or "Won't you please attend my reception at-" type of message those people are always sending each other.

"Charles Trumble?"

"Trumbo."

The messenger flicks a smidge of dust from his immaculate uniform, obviously put-off with this required visit to the rather dirty and smelly lower crew decks. The Special Courier promises himself a nice hot aromatic bath after coming all the way down here to deliver a message to this obvious dredge of onboard humanity.

He sniffs through raised nostrils and raises his tablet, announcing that the message he is about to read is from none other than Captain Richard Cable, Commander of the very large and expensive passenger liner on which Chuck is so fortunate to have a job.

"The message follows: 'To the attention of fourth-class shipman, er, ship-person, Charles F. Trumble—'"

"Trumbo."

"What?"

"Trumbo. Charles Trumbo."

The Special Courier checks his display. "Ah yes, of course. 'Trumbo'. We'll get that corrected." He reads on, his monotone reflecting his intense disinterest. "It has come to the attention of the executive of this vessel that you are about to receive several university degrees and the order of Docturus Emeritus Meritus cum laude. Congratulations, fellow shipmate for a job well done. The awards ceremony will be held at a special dinner at the Captain's Table on Tuesday night promptly at seven in the evening. Proper attire is required, and you may bring one guest."

"Proper attire?"

The messenger sniffs again, looking Chuck up and down. "Wear..." he evaluates Chuck's frumpy clothes and lifts his nose so high Chuck can clearly see into his forward sinus, "...something decent." With that, the man turns on his heels.

The Special Courier speeds away, leaving Chuck with a white, square envelope with the janitor's name embossed on the front. The contents confirm every word the courier said. He, Charles Trumbo (even though it says "Trumble") is invited to the Captain's Table and he may bring one guest.

A quick communication locates Violet. Now, all Chuck can think is how proud Violet will be when he shows her the invitation. He practically runs to the transports and catches an express up to the Pool and Sauna Luxury area on Upper Deck 23.

He shows his Maintenance badge which gets him into the pool area, one of the most opulent decks on the ship. The place looks worthy of a Roman emperor, with stately columns holding up the ceiling which resembles a sumptuous ancient palace. All around the pool, passengers are being waited-on hand and foot, literally. Hand massages, foot rubs, and everything in between are being administered as the passengers sip expensive drinks through long, thin straws. Every drink has an umbrella in it.

Three guests run across the deck in front of Chuck, screaming "Geronimo!" and leaping into the deep blue water. A massive splash catches Chuck and there is much laughter all around the pool as the revelers surface, whooping with inebriated joy.

Chuck tries to avoid the edge of the pool as he searches for Violet. Without warning, a squirt of water hits him in the right ear. "Hey," he shouts.

A mischievous snicker comes from behind one of the deck chairs and Chuck spies a little girl in a pink bathing suit with multi-colored balloons printed on it and water wings on each arm. She's holding an oversized squirt gun.

"Did you—?"

Before he can finish the question, he gets his answer in a face-full stream of plastic-smelling water. The squirt gun lights up and emits realistic phasor sounds.

"Stop it, you little brat. Go bother someone else." He spins and starts off toward the sauna area. He's drilled in the back of his head with a long squirt. That cute little snicker blends with more weapon blasts.

Chuck escapes to the Adults Only area. The place is meant to resemble the palace of some ancient decadent Roman emperor and it does a pretty fair job. Purple cloths hang like togas on decorative stone columns and everything is done up in white marble with touches of gold leaf.

Just as Chuck is about to enter the pool office to enquire about Violet, he hears a commanding voice, "Achilles, tell the men to put it down there. No, not there, here. '*Alla*'…I mean '*aqui*.'" There's no mistaking the delicate tone of Violet, even if she is calling out commands like a boxer's coach.

Chuck rounds one of the Roman columns and sees Violet standing on the pool deck, directing a work party of men moving a seven-foot-tall urn. The thing must weigh a ton as it's taking six men to move it this way and one large man standing back, shouting translated instructions as Violet tries to get them to maneuver the monstrosity into just the right place.

The foreman shouts instructions to his men, "*Nao! Nao tao longe. Volta! Volta!*"

"Violet? May I speak with you?"

"Sure, Chuck, go ahead. No!" This startles him speechless. Violet is looking up, sternly giving commands to the workers. "To the right. Right, not left."

"*O Que?*"

"Well," Chuck begins again, "er, the thing is…"

"To the right! Do I have to come up there myself?"

"*O Que?* What, Miss Violet?" asks Achilles, the foreman.

"Um…" murmurs Chuck.

Achilles lets loose a string of words, but these are aimed more at his own men. "*Esta mulher estÁ louca?*" The workers grin at each other.

During the pause, Violet turns to Chuck. "Go ahead, Chuck."

"Well," says Chuck, waving the little envelope, "the thing is, I've been invited to the Captain's Dinner–"

"Oh, that's great Chuck, what are they having? Fine, now push it forward."

"Oh well, I'm not sure. The thing is…um, Violet? Would you like to…"

"No!"

"Oh," Chuck says, a little put out.

"Push, Achilles, not pull. Push."

Achilles lets loose a screaming torrent, "*A mulher disse, empurre, nao puxe, seu idiota, empurre!*"

"I can see you're kind of busy."

"Oh, I'm sorry, Chuck. They sent a Brazilian work party this time and forgot to include a Portuguese translator. Do you speak any Portuguese, Chuck?"

Chuck almost misses her meaning as he finds himself once again entranced by her flashing green eyes and ringlets of dark hair. "Oh, um no," he recovers, "That's alright. Why don't you just get back to–"

"Wait, no. What was that about the Captain?"

Chuck gushes out the whole idea before something else happens to distract her, "WillyougototheCaptainsdinner…I mean, with me?"

Violet smiles and her smile dazzles Chuck so profoundly for several moments he doesn't realize she has accepted his invite. He even has trouble finding his way out of the pool area.

Behind him, Achilles shouts more orders, "*Nao, nao, para o outro lado!*" but Chuck walks away in a daze. He barely hears Violet calling up to the workers and Achilles' cry of, "*Parre! Parre!*"

Chuck has no clue that, one minute after he leaves, the huge flower urn will topple off its high pedestal, not only smashing into uncountable pieces, but putting a large hole in the otherwise perfect granite deck surrounding the luxury pool.

Chapter Fourteen

Green Terror

The two technicians make their way deep into the belly of the ship. Pipes emit hissing and humming as precious fluids and gases circulate through the huge ship. These two are unlucky enough to have drawn the unenvied "short straw" and the duty of inspecting "The Devils". Those of you familiar with sailing ships of ancient Earth sea-going vessels may already know the concept of a ship's "Devil". On those ships, one huge beam of wood ran from stem to stern, being the backbone of the whole assembly. This beam was also the place most vulnerable to springing leaks. In those olden days, the worst duty a crewman could draw was to "have the Devil to pay", the despicable duty of carrying a bucket of hot tar to the deepest, smelliest parts of the ship and applying the tar where leaks threatened.

Now, centuries later, the duty still exists with many changes. There are now seven "Devils", each needing the careful inspection of human eyes. Instead of buckets of tar, the men now carry high-tech glue guns with Forever Epoxy (registered trademark) to seal the hull.

The one thing that has not changed: it's still the deepest, darkest, smelliest place on the ship. The Zap-DU is a close second. Most robots break down or get stuck and there are a few that simply refuse to stoop so low. So, it's these brave men who face the hazards to climb through the muck to inspect the Devils and fill in tiny cracks before they become emergencies.

Today the two techs crawling through the hatch leading to one of the "Devils" are Second-Class Engineering Technicians Tennyson and Lightwing.

"Don't push," Tennyson snarls, "I'm getting there as fast as I can. My gawd it stinks. Can't they put a filter in these suits?"

"Quit yer moanin', pal," says Lightwing. His voice sounds funny as he is doing almost all his breathing through his mouth. "We're almost done for the day. Two more hours and we can be in a nice hot shower."

"Ah, I think I'm snagged on something."

Lightwing raises his light, "Yeah, I see it. You left one of the tightening straps loose. When ya gonna learn?" He reaches up, slips the loop free, and tucks it in. "Your turn to do the far end. I'll start here and we'll meet in the middle. Keep your communicator on."

"Why?" asks Tennyson, "I get sick of listening to you sing."

"For one thing," says Lightwing, "It's regulations. For another, I can sing okay. Better'n you."

Tennyson scoffs and starts his half-crawl to the other end of the Devil. "I hate this," he grumbles, "Mom wanted me to be a stockbroker but, 'No', I says like I knew anything.

I had to go and join the Space Force. Next thing I know, they've got me loading freighters and busting my butt for hundred-forty credits a week."

Lightwing's voice crackles over his headset, "Yeah, yeah, I know. Is this the version where you say, 'It's a cryin' shame what I've become' or the version where you says, 'I coulda been a CEO?'"

"Don't laugh at me. I got good grades. Top marks. Just didn't have the money to get into Finance College. So, it was the dregs for me, remedial pre-college and then the Space Force."

"Don't you ever talk about anything else, Tennyson? What about birds? Tell me about one o' them hot college girls you dated."

Tennyson has to struggle over a large mound of detritus and steps down into a spongy substance. He almost hates to look down, fearing he might see something sticky and smelly on his boot. What he sees is quite different. It seems his foot has landed on a smooth green carpet, a spotted, rubbery surface stretching from one side of the narrow corridor, over the Devil to the other wall. The carpet ends about ten meters away and all along the edge of the carpet are long, green rods. But it's what's in the center of the carpet that captures Tennyson's entire attention.

Rising up from the exact middle of the large rubber rug is a stack of glass bottles, each glistening with tiny shards of ice. Tennyson's headlamp light reflects off the bottles, the light revealing that, under their coating of ice, the bottles are the dark brown hue of the classic beer bottle.

"Beer," whispers Tennyson.

"What's that," asks Lightwing, "You're breaking up."

"Lightwing, I found beer."

"You found what? Did you say you got something in your ear?"

Tennyson's voice is quiet with awe. "It's a miracle", he says.

"Tennyson, are you alright?"

Tennyson's next outburst gets Lighwing moving toward him, "If you don't hurry, buddy, I'm gonna drink it all."

Running, crawling, and climbing over mounds of smelly things, Lightwing tries to keep his light pointed ahead. "Tennyson, you'd better wait for me." He hears Tennyson laugh in such a way that tells him he'll be lucky to get a taste. "Tennyson."

Up ahead, Lightwing sees Tennyson's light jerk toward the ceiling and hears a slight "Erk!" As he tops a particularly high mound, Lightwing comes to a spot where he has a full view but it's not at all what Tennyson saw from the same vantage.

What Lightwing sees is a great green rubbery thing folded up like a taco. Along the edges of each side are sharp-looking stems, crossing like eyelashes. In between these he sees Tennyson's hand sticking out, frantically waving.

"Get me out of here," shouts Tennyson, his voice muffled by the huge green trap.

Lightwing realizes the voice is not coming over the communicator but from inside. "Tennyson, is that you?"

"Get me out of here. As soon as I touched the beer, this thing grabbed me."

Lightwing runs up and grabs the two sides of the lips, avoiding a couple of nasty green spikes. But when he tries to pull the lips apart, his grip slips and he comes away with a slick, oily substance on his hands. Immediately, his skin starts itching furiously.

"I can't pull it apart," yells Lightwing.

"Do something. I'm starting to itch all over." Tennyson sounds completely panicked.

"I think I need to go get help," shouts Lightwing.

"Don't leave me," begs Tennyson, "I think I can push my arm out further." Sure enough, Tennyson's hand stretches a few inches further, exposing most of his forearm.

Lightwing gasps and involuntarily steps away. Tennyson's hand is now beet-red and swelling but, worse than that, the protective clothing of his sleeve is eaten away, starting to completely fall apart. Lightwing realizes the oily liquid is acidic, even as his own hands start to burn rather than itch.

He takes the man's hand in his and is at once shocked at how desperately strong Tennyson's grip is on him. "Look, man, I've got to get someone to help me free you."

"Can't you try again? My skin is starting to burn." Tennyson wails, "Try something. Maybe hit it with something big."

Lightwing spies a rusted old piece of pipe lying in the muck at his feet. "Found something," he hollers, and then, "Tennyson, you have to let go of my hand so I can reach it."

"Alright," comes the muffled reply but it still takes a moment for the man to release his hand.

Lightwing takes the pipe and moves to the side of the thing. He decides to aim low, assuming that he'll have to damage the base of the trap to force it to let go. He pulls back and swings with all his might.

The pipe rebounds off the surface like he's just swung and hit an old rubber tire. "Ow," screams Tennyson, "You son-of-a-bug-eater, I think you broke my leg."

Lightwing steps back and thinks for a minute. He jams the pipe in between the lips, just below Tennyson's hand, and tries to wedge the sides open. Instead of the lips parting, the pipe starts to bend.

"It's too strong. I can't get the edges apart." He waits, expecting another plea from Tennyson, but the man doesn't answer.

"Tennyson? Can you hear me?"

"Yes, I…hear you…" Tennyson's voice is very weak. He sounds out-of-it.

"Tennyson? You've got to hang in there. Stay strong."

"Lightwing, can you…tell my mother something?"

"No, Tennyson," Lightwing cries, "You can tell her yourself when you get out of there." But his words ring hollow, even to himself.

"Tell…my mother…I love her."

Lightwing realizes the man is fading fast. "Anything else?"

"You…owe me money…"

Despite several more exhortations, that's the last Lightwing hears from Tennyson.

Lightwing steps back horrified at what he's just seen. Then, the last straw as he sees Tennyson's hand slowly being swallowed between the lips.

Suddenly the plant gives a loud *BURP*, startling Lightwing. He backs up a step and finds he's crowded up against the mound of detritus he climbed to get here. Suddenly the space feels even more hot and confined.

I've got to get out of here, he thinks. Hesitant to turn his back on the green monstrosity, he climbs up the mound, fearing he might be grabbed at any minute. When he reaches the top, he points his light back down the maintenance corridor. He gasps.

A smaller green rubbery-looking carpet stretches about two meters wide, partially blocking his escape, and seems to be getting larger every second. In the center, Lightwing can make out a rough shape forming on a stalk in the center of the thing, vaguely resembling a bottle of beer.

Chapter Fifteen

Dr. Picaldy's New Patient

"Hi Doc," Roswell greets her, "any interesting new patients?" The Chief has a look of triumph on his face that reminds Picaldy of Nero looking down on Rome in flames.

"I know you think you made your point, Chief, but there has to be another explanation besides," Picaldy drops her voice to a whisper, "aliens."

Roswell chortles, "Oh, of course. Lots of reasons why everything liquid might be drained from the body of our crewman."

Picaldy's face reddens, "I'm not saying I don't care what happened to him, I'm just saying I don't think the cause was…that."

The Chief tightens his jaw, huffing a bit, "I suppose you agree with the Padre's crazy notion."

"The Padre? What does he say?"

"Oh, you two haven't been colluding?"

"Roswell, keep a civil tongue. As officer to officer, I can tell you the Padre and I have no secrets we're keeping from you."

"Alright, Doc. I'm sorry. At times like this, you don't know who to trust."

"Well, I warn you against letting paranoia get control. From a medical standpoint, that's just as dangerous as hysteria. Now, what's the Padre's theory?"

Roswell pulls the Doctor into a side passage and waits for a young man in a mechanic's uniform to pass by. In a hoarse whisper, "He blames vampires."

For a moment, the Doctor is speechless, evaluating what she's has just heard. Then her laughter echoes down the empty corridor, "Vampires?"

Two ladies from the Personal Care deck, sitting at the end of the corridor, look up from their lunch.

Roswell is both trying to quieten the Doctor and failing to suppress his own laughter. "I know…I know…shh… That's some crazy stuff, huh? Look we'd better be quiet. Even something that outrageous could start a panic."

Continuing to snicker, the Doctor says, "Look here, Chief, I've got a few calls to make. What say we get together tomorrow for breakfast?"

Just as the Chief is about to accept the invite, his communicator buzzes. Roswell holds up one finger to Picaldy before taking the call. "What is it, Phillips?"

"Sir, I hate to bother you with this, but I've got one of the techs here telling me a really crazy story. Apparently, he saw something that scared him out of his shorts, and he lost his work partner at the same time."

"Well, throw him in a cell until he sobers up."

"See, that's the thing, sir. He has injuries that seem to bear out his story."

"Injuries?" Picaldy's head snaps around. "Okay, Phillips," says Roswell, "Where are you?"

"Sick Bay, sir. The man just won't calm down."

"Keep him there, Phillips. Doctor Picaldy and I will be right down."

"Up, sir. We're on Upper Deck 25."

"Right, we'll be right there." He clicks off. "Doc, you'd better come with me. We've got an injured man who claims to have seen something."

As they hurry off together, they fail to hear one of the Personal Care ladies say to the other, "Did he say 'vampires'?"

Second-Class Engineering Specialist Lightwing sits trembling on one of the examination beds. He has a blanket draped over his shoulders and cradles a mug of steaming Joe, but still, he's shaking like an Aspen leaf as the Chief, Phillips, and Doctor Picaldy come in. A nurse goes up to them, flipping open a medical tablet and pointing to the man's vitals.

"He came in here about half an hour ago, babbling incoherently. His heart was racing, and he nearly passed out twice. Shock, I'd say."

Doctor Picaldy takes over. "Thank you, nurse. I'll take it from here. So, young man, how're you feeling?"

Lightwing looks up and opens his mouth to speak. Instead, he gulps and coughs, seemingly unable to form the words.

"Come on now, Steven," says the nurse, "This is Doctor Picaldy. She's here to help you." She gently places her hand on his back and uses her other hand to straighten him up a bit. "Just take a deep breath. Come on, deep breath."

Lightwing takes in a shuddering breath and huffs it out. The second one is longer, slower, calmer.

"There," says the nurse, "Better?" He nods. "Now just tell these folks what you saw in your own words."

He looks furtively to each as if to see if they are already laughing at him. "It's Tennyson. I think he's dead. This thing…this big green thing…ate him."

Roswell glances at the other two and starts to speak but Picaldy puts a hand up to stop him. "Go on, son," she says in her gentlest bedside voice.

Lightwing swallows hard. "We was cleaning and sealing Devil Seven, on Lower 150. Two more hours and we'd be at the bar, drinkin' and bitchin'."

Phillips lets out a choked laugh but sharp looks from the Chief and Picaldy shut him up quick.

"So, it was Tennyson's turn to start at the far side. That's how we do it. One guy goes all the way out and we meet in the middle. It kinda like gives us a goal, you know?"

They nod and Roswell resists the urge to tell him to get on with it.

"So, all of a sudden I hear Tennyson say he's found beer."

"What?" All three can't help but let the exclamation out.

"I know, sir, I know. It sounded crazy to me too. But then Tennyson starts laughing, telling me he's gonna drink it all before I can get there. Well, sir, begging you officers' pardon but I couldn't hardly let him get it all. I start running…well, moving quick as I can, climbing all over the crap that's in my way. So, finally, I get to where Tennyson is but instead of the guy sitting there, drinkin' a brew, he's like being..." Lightwing can barely get the word out, "swallowed."

"Swallowed?" says Chief Roswell, "Swallowed by what?" In an instant, the Chief's idea of what the aliens might look like has radically altered. Suddenly he sees them as giants, huge green creatures with mouths large enough to swallow a man whole.

"What did it look like?" asks the Doctor but Lightwing has gone back to shaking, obviously re-living the terrible moment. "Son," Picaldy says, "you've got to tell us what it looked like."

Lightwing stares up at the Doc with wide, terrified eyes. "It...looked..." he says between shivers, "like...a giant ... green...taco." He crumples up in a fetal position and gasps, "Oh gawd, it was terrible."

Doctor Picaldy turns to the other officers. "We have to let him rest. I'll talk to him again once he's had a chance to get himself together. Nurse, see that he sleeps and gets something to eat, will you? Gentlemen, let's go into the other room."

"Beer? Tacos?" says Phillips, "Sirs, I'd say those men were already in the bag while they were working. Give me a few minutes with them and I'll have them confessing."

"Them, Phillips? We only have one of them."

"The other one's probably sleeping it off in one of the storerooms," sneers Phillips.

"I wouldn't be so sure," says Chief Roswell, "Phillips, I want you to lead a search party down to that area. What did he say, Devil Seven or something? Take an armed security team and find that other man. Tennyson, right? Find Tennyson."

"But, Chief," protests Phillips.

"I mean it, man, get cracking."

Phillips stalks off, muttering about hysterical drunken crewmen.

"Well?" says the Doctor, "What do you make of it?"

"Seems obvious to me," says Roswell, "They're infiltrating, somehow getting aboard without being detected, just as I suspected."

"The aliens." The Doctor shakes her head. "Couldn't it be something else? Maybe we picked up some bad beer at our last port-o-call. These men might have gotten some alien beer or something. Made them hallucinate. I could see that."

"Oh, really, Doctor? Bad beer? That's your theory? Then how do you explain both men seeing the same hallucination?"

Chapter Sixteen

The Captain's Table

When Chuck arrives at her cabin, Violet looks like a model just stepping off the cover of *DASH* magazine. Indeed, Chuck is so completely stunned by her looks he forgets to hand her the flowers until she reaches for them.

"Oh, you got me *Rosa kordesii*!"

"No, these are just roses. Um, here you go."

As she takes them, she gives Chuck a sly smile. "What are you trying to say?"

"Um, 'thanks for going with me to the dinner'?"

She laughs. "No silly. The rose you chose. They're amphidiploids."

He stares blankly, then, "They are?"

"Oh, I get it. How sweet. You think we should have triplets."

"What? No, I don't."

"Your mouth says 'no,'" Violet says, "but your choice of rose says yes. Let me put them in water."

Before they leave, Violet pins one of the perky blooms on Chuck's lapel. "There, that does it. You look wonderful."

When they reach the executive dining room, Violet and Chuck are met by a slim waiter in a tuxedo who shows them into a well-appointed lounge with an expansive bar taking up most of one wall. Every woman present is wearing their best evening gown and the men are all puffed up in penguin suits and fancy dress. Chuck's awfully glad Violet made him rent the black suit and bow tie.

"Excuse me." A young officer with an athletic physique confronts Chuck. "You may have the wrong event. This is the Captain's Table. You must be looking for the crew's mess hall."

Before Chuck can say anything, a tall, whiskered man in a perfect uniform, decorations glistening and ribbons streaming, steps up to Violet.

"Well, if it isn't my little flower tender. How are you, my dear?"

Violet sets her jaw and allows him to buss her cheek but pulls back quickly lest he linger.

"Captain Cable, I'd like you to meet my boyfriend, Charles Trumbo."

The captain gives him an appraising once over. "How are you, young man?"

Chuck is a bit speechless. This is, after all, a captain of the Dwarf Star Cruise Line, the highest-ranking officer on the ship. The thought occurs to Chuck that he is way out of his league. He finally pulls out the invitation and mumbles, "I was invited…"

"What's that?" asks the captain and takes the envelope. Reading the invitation, he bursts out, "Well of course you were, young Trumble. I had no idea I was speaking with the guest of honor." He raps the bar to get everyone's attention. "Ladies and gentlemen, ladies and gentlemen. I am indeed pleased to present tonight's guest of honor, Doctor Charles Trumble."

Before Chuck can say it, Violet says forcefully, "Trumbo."

The captain misses this as he calls out, "Drinks. Everyone, get a drink. My dear, what are you having?"

Violet orders a Gin Fizz and Chuck gets an orange juice.

"A toast, everyone. I toast tonight's guest of honor, here to receive multiple degrees from the Ultra Long-Distance University, one of our own," the captain glances at the invitation and reads, "Fourth-class Maintenance Specialist Charles Trumble."

Violet fairly shouts, "Trumbo," but the cry is drowned out in a loud toast by everyone present.

Chuck has never been introduced to so many people at once and certainly has never heard the word 'Congratulations' repeated to him so often. The only thing is, that young officer is shooting very direct and dirty looks at him. Chuck can't, for the life of him, figure out what he might have done to anger the man so. Finally, the man circles in to be introduced.

"Ah," says the captain, "Allow me to introduce my First Officer, Rhett Reynolds. Officer Reynolds, our guest of honor Charles Trumble."

Chuck starts to correct him, but Reynolds speaks first. "So, the Janitor Genius, isn't that what people are calling you?"

Chuck frowns, "I haven't heard that one."

The captain offers a loud laugh. "Watch out, Reynolds. This one isn't going to remain a janitor long. You might be talking to the next Dwarf Star captain." Everyone laughs, everyone but Chuck, who is surprised to hear his dream come from the mouth of the captain, and Reynolds whose glare seems even darker.

Finally, the handshaking and the small talk comes to an end as the ringing of a small bell quietens the crowd. The head waiter announces, "Dinner is served."

Violet feels the captain take her arm. "This way, my dear, you and Charles have the seats next to mine. He leads her to sit directly to his right and points Chuck to the next seat down.

"Oh, Captain," says Violet, "You're mistaken. The guest of honor should be next to you."

"What's that," harrumphs the captain.

"The placard definitely says Chuck should be seated here." She starts to get up, but Captain Cable is quick to press her back down and snatches up the little card. He quickly switches the 'Charles Trumbo' card with the 'Violet Dewberry' one.

"Sorry about the mix-up," he says, glaring at the head waiter, "you just can't get good help these days."

The first course is served, and everyone digs into their salad.

"So, Trumble," says Captain Cable, "tell us about your studies. Pass the dressing, please. You certainly fooled everyone. Your superiors didn't mention your rather expansive intellectual capabilities."

Everyone looks at Chuck, but he heard no question in that statement. However, it's evident that people are waiting for him to speak.

"Well…um…I just studied hard. I mean I worked on it when I had the chance, you know."

"Oh yes," says the Captain, beaming, "Every spare moment, I'd imagine. Goodness, engine mechanics, music theory, physics, and even navigation? Quite commendable."

The diners mumble their approval between bites of kale, jicama, and watercress. Finally, Reynolds can stand no more of this. "So, how did you, a Fourth Classman, how did you do it? The sheer number of hours required seems more than you would have had available with your work schedule."

Chuck realizes the man, as First Officer, is second in command of the great ship. He pales a little. "I…I mostly studied at night."

"At night? Well, it must have been difficult not to get any sleep for the last few weeks. You must be very tired."

Chuck relaxes, "Oh yes, of course, sir. Tired."

Violet smiles admiringly and there is a general agreeable murmur around the table in between bites of crunchy greens.

"So tired you might make mistakes in your regular work?" The First Officer smiles evilly, happy to finally pin down this miscreant. "I believe there was an incident?"

"Well, um…" Chuck is at a loss for words. They both glance over at the Captain, the First Officer hoping to see an accusatory expression on his superior's face.

But the Captain, completely unaware of what has been said, is sloppily whispering something into the ear of our cute botanist who seems rather shocked by whatever he is suggesting. The table gets quiet enough for all to hear the last four whispered words, "...up to my quarters."

The First Officer clears his throat, and the Captain looks around. "How is everyone's salad?"

Everyone immediately comments on the delightful greens, crisp lettuce, juicy tomatoes, and what was that dressing? The waiters move in and replace salad bowls with the next savory course.

There is a small interruption as Security Chief Roswell arrives in his dress uniform.

"Terribly sorry to arrive late, Captain," he says, "Couldn't be avoided. A little trouble down in Engineering." He nods to the table, "Good evening, everyone." His eyes fall on Chuck. "Good evening, young man. I'm a bit surprised to see you...up here."

Before Chuck can reply, the captain says, "Not at all, Roswell. Charles is our guest of honor."

"Indeed? Well, good for you, young man, good for you."

"But, really," presses the First Officer Reynolds again as the waiters place a veal piccata smothered with tomato sauce and a thick, yellow cheese. "For instance, the hours required to memorize the Tables of Navigation alone. How could you squeeze it in with all your other drib-drab duties?"

Chuck's sweat runs down his back. Now he'll get caught and he'll be embarrassed in front of all of them, most of all Violet. "I...um...well, memorizing's not all that hard. You just read it over and over—"

"Yes, yes," the captain interrupts, "See here, haven't we had enough of this line of conversation? He doesn't have to take the tests twice, Reynolds." There is a general round of laughter at First Officer Reynolds' expense.

Reynolds smiles wanly, his face turning a bit red although one could not tell if this is from embarrassment or anger. "Yes, Captain, I just thought Fourth-Class Trumble—"

"Trumbo," Violet corrects.

"Trumbo," snaps Reynolds, "If the *janitor* might regale us with perhaps reciting the General Theory of Stardrive?" Reynolds gives Chuck an I've-got-you-now look.

"Good heavens, Reynolds," snaps Captain Cable, "we're eating, for Gawd's sake. Why don't you let the man enjoy his moment of victory? If I didn't know better, I'd say you were jealous." Some of the attendees let out little snickers of suppressed laughter.

"Jealous, sir?" Reynolds is incredulous. "Of...of *this?*"

The captain adjusts his napkin. In his best Captain's-giving-an-order voice, he says "First Officer Reynolds, do I have to order you to be a gentleman?"

Reynolds lowers his head, "No, Captain."

"Now that we have that settled," says the captain, "I'd like to propose another toast. I am informed that our accomplished Fourth-Class crewman Charles *Trumbo*, has at his side the very lovely Second-Class botanist, Violet Dewberry. To Miss Dewberry."

"Miss Dewberry," the diners chant and tip their glasses.

The dinner progresses rather smoothly through the main course. Conversation remains light and easy, mostly consisting of the captain's account of the pranks he pulled when a young man. Doctor Picaldy tells a hilarious medical joke, the one about the time a sperm met a protozoa, and so on.

Chuck does find he must avoid nasty stares from First Officer Reynolds when no one else is looking. The smoldering expression telegraphs a level of hate from the man that makes swallowing his veal a little difficult.

Chuck prefers to bask in Violet's admiring glow. More than once she whispers how proud she is of him. Unlike Chuck, Violet is able to carry on conversations with almost everyone at the table, asking questions, tittering with laughter at their little jokes.

To Chuck's surprise, Reynolds is addressing him in a polite tone.

"You know, Trumble—"

"*TRUMBO*," Violet corrects, a little too forcibly.

"Yes, of course," says Reynolds in a completely unapologetic manner, "I was just saying, I was first in my class in Navigation School. We used to have competitions to see who could navigate the best."

Chuck nods and says, "That's nice. This veal is great, isn't it, everyone?"

There is a general round of appreciations, compliments, and toasts to the chef. The captain excuses himself to go to the lavatory.

"Well, janitor?" Reynolds' voice cuts across the jovial murmur as soon as the captain is out of earshot, "What do you say?"

The table falls quiet. Chuck frowns, "What's that?"

Reynolds takes on a deadly aspect. "I challenge you to a Navigation Duel. A three-star, two black hole, fourteen planet trip using Blanchard's precepts, lowest circum-navigatory time wins."

Every eye turns to Chuck. It's all he can do to keep himself from wilting like a tulip in a heat wave. Then he catches Violet's look. She is smiling, exuding all the confidence in him he doesn't feel in himself. He hears his mouth say the words, "I accept."

Reynolds returns to his triumphant smile, "More wine?"

They all look up to the Captain who has returned to the table. Captain Cable is lost in thought and is, just at that moment, concentrating on Violet's chest, trying to get a good look at her cleavage and arguing with himself whether hers are bigger than his manicurist's.

"What? Oh, er...yes of course. More wine. Carry on, men."

When this response brings only confused murmurs from the delegates at the table, the Captain quickly regains his composure, raises his glass, and says, "A toast."

The guests quickly raise their glasses and look at him expectantly.

"To our shipmate....um, where is it?" The First Officer reluctantly pulls out a framed diploma and hands it to the captain. "Oh, ah yes. To the new Doctor Charles Trumbo."

The guests, save the First Officer, all join in, "To Doctor Trumbo."

The Captain smiles, Violet beams, the table cheers (in a quiet respectable manner), and the First Officer glares triumphantly at Chuck, who looks worried, confused, and bashful all at the same time.

Chapter Seventeen

A Kiss Under the Stars

After the dinner, Chuck and Violet walk slowly toward the transporters, laughing about the dinner and all the funny things people said or did. She's full of praise and asks to see his new diplomas again. He opens the thin black box holding them and she is cooing with pride as the transporter arrives.

"I have an idea." Violet's eyes glisten with excitement. "It's too early just to go home. Have you ever seen the Arboretum?"

Chuck nods. "We wax the lobby every few weeks. It's one of the areas we have to clean the glass but that's just once a year. We always do that when we're in station."

She smiles. "It sounds like you've never visited and just walked around the gardens."

"I guess not."

"So," she says, a mischievous look playing across her features, "I *know* you've never been there at night."

"At night? It's closed at night. I mean, you know, during nighttime hours."

"Chuck, I'm a botanist. I'm in charge of the health of every plant on board this ship."

He frowns a little. "So?"

"So, of course, I have a keycard."

"Oh."

They stroll along the verdant paths and Violet points out the various blooming fronds, reeling off the Latin names, pointing out which ones are in the same scientific family. The vast canopy of stars above them, made so visible by the low nighttime lights, is breathtaking. Violet starts to point out a few important stars but then laughs at herself.

"But you already know these, don't you?" she says, her admiration igniting her bright green eyes.

He murmurs something and gives her a weak smile. She takes his hand, and they cross a pretty little bridge where an artificial waterfall pours into a small pond. This path takes visitors to the equatorial plants section. Here the air is warm, and the grounds teem with life. One can almost hear the rolling waves and imagine a beach nearby and the great jungle beyond.

"Let's sit here," she says. They sit together on a lovely, molded bench and Chuck is pleased when Violet snuggles up against him.

"I'm very happy, Chuck," she says.

"Me too."

She catches him looking at her lips.

"Oh, Chuck, I'm so proud of you."

"Really? Well, I didn't do much."

"Oh really? That's so cute."

"What?"

"You want to kiss me."

"I do? Oh yes, I do."

They kiss. Chuck is thinking this should be the greatest moment in his life. This should be when he finally feels the sweet surrender of love. It should be when he realizes how far he's come in just a few weeks. It should be…but it isn't.

Surrounding them on every side are all manner of tropical green plant. Huge ferns, winding vines, coconut trees, and hanging greenery which would normally be perceived as relaxing and comforting to the casual visitor now feel too close, crowding in on the two of them. Chuck feels a wave of dread. Maybe it's the vines lying across the ground or the broad leaves, but everywhere he looks, Chuck sees the Plant. It's as if the ghost of his dead "little buddy" is staring back at him, accusing him.

Violet feels this change through the kiss. "What's the matter, Chuck?" she asks.

"I…oh, nothing." He pulls her into a hug, so she won't see him studying the huge plants around them.

My imagination is just playing tricks on me, he thinks fiercely, *there's nothing there. I put the Plant in the disposer. It's gone.*

Still, the trembling plants surrounding them seem filled with a million accusing eyes.

"Violet?"

"Yes?" she says dreamily, snuggling a little deeper into his embrace.

"Can we go?"

"What?" She pulls back a little to look into his eyes. "What's the matter?"

"It's my leg. It's cramping a bit. Must have been sitting too long."

"Chuck. We've only been sitting here a few minutes."

"I know but…oof." He stands suddenly, doing a good job faking a leg cramp.

"Oh," exclaims Violet, "are you alright?"

"Yeah, I just need to walk it off."

Violet stands up, smoothing out her nice dress. "Fine. I need to be getting to bed soon. Busy day tomorrow." She starts walking back down the path toward the transporters. "Coming?"

Even Chuck can tell she's a little miffed. "I'm sorry, Violet, I really am." How can he tell her, of all people, the plants were freaking him out…and why?

As they walk away, they fail to notice the plants tremble even though the air is still.

Chapter Eighteen

Science for Dummies

Captain Cable, hearing about more of the crew disappearing, demands answers.

"I don't know what's going on, Roswell. That's what I pay you for."

"Yes, sir."

"You've got one last chance. Get out there and come back with some answers."

"Yes, Captain."

Captain Cable is about to dismiss him when he gets an idea. Roswell can tell because the man is suddenly smiling, and his eyebrows are jumping up and down. "Tell you what you do," says the captain excitedly, "Get together the brightest minds, all those science department heads. Get them in one place and make them give you some answers."

If it were strictly up to him, Security Chief Roswell would leave the scientists in their labs where they prefer to stay. But the captain's orders are clear…very clear.

A few short hours later, the Chief is winding up a review of all the happenings (at least the ones he's willing to reveal to these eggheads). The scientists are sworn to secrecy except among themselves, but Roswell has little faith they'll keep quiet.

Roswell winds up his presentation. "So that's where we stand. Seven engineering crew, two cadets, three passengers, and four kitchen staff are missing. The little evidence we've been able to recover is on those tables behind you. So far, the perpetrators have eluded us. The Dwarf Star Cruise Company, who by the way signs your paychecks, wants you to figure out who, or what is doing this."

The Chief gives them a few minutes but the murmurs around the room tell him nothing.

"Look, I want one of you to explain…at least take an educated guess…about what's going on here." Several scientists begin to speak at once. Roswell holds his hands up, "I said one of you."

A couple of them look at an older scientist with wiry gray hair sticking up from a mostly bald pate. "What about Doctor Marshall?"

Another bespectacled, thin scientist shakes his head, "Not Marshall. His discipline is molecular resonance. How is that going to help us?"

"Oh," quips a short scientist in a rumpled jacket, "and I suppose you'd like to nominate yourself as spokesman—"

"Person," snaps a large female scientist with horn-rimmed glasses, "Gawd, you men are so sexist."

Rumpled Jacket speaks up again, "Person, then. But really, Polk has no place speaking for the rest of us either."

"I beg your pardon?" says the one with wiry gray hair, Dr. Polk, "I'll have you know I once addressed the entire assemblage of the Interdisciplinary Council."

"Oh, really? What were you accused of?" quips Marshall. This is followed by a round of nasty laughter at Polk's expense.

"Stop this," shouts Roswell, using his I'm-going-to-give-you-such-a-licking voice. "Stop it right now or I'm going to throw you all in the brig." This shuts the scientists up quite efficiently. "Now," says Roswell in his I'm-being-reasonable-for-the-moment voice, "I want one of you to explain what you think is going on."

Most of them look to Doctor Marshall as Dr. Polk just stands aside, pouting.

"Alright, then," says Doctor Marshall, "The day this all happened, when the thing caused the huge machine to stop. It was misidentified as a rock but then the analysis computer correctly identified this ersatz rock as a seed."

"Yes, yes," says Roswell impatiently, "we already know that."

"Well, shortly thereafter, Captain Cable issued the gag order, so the entire analysis report was labeled as 'Top Secret' and none of us were allowed to see it until yesterday."

"And?"

Rumpled Jacket pipes up, "The computer tried to warn us."

Several heads nod and the scientists launch into multiple conversations. Roswell holds up a hand, "One voice," he says looking at Marshall.

"Ah, hmm, yes," Dr. Marshall assumes his professorial lecture tone, "Well, the analysis computer's report warned us that the seed was from one of three dangerous plants. It could either be the Giant Tickleberry, the Climbing Horsefly Trap, or in the worst case, a *Sticklyus chameleonica gigantica.*"

"So?" says Roswell, "What does all this mean? In simple layman's language, please."

"If it is revealed to be the Tickleberry bush then the most serious calamity we might face is a bunch of crewmen, er, I mean persons, giggling like morons. Although this plant *can* interfere with operations, it's doubtful anyone would be harmed.

"The Horsefly Trap will climb and be an annoyance, wrapping itself around critical pieces of equipment, that sort of thing. But its traps are rather obvious," he chuckles as do several of the others, "and easily avoidable."

He glances around at the other scientists, and they nod, encouraging their colleague. "But if instead we somehow have scooped up a seed from the *Sticklyus chameleonica gigantica*, then we are faced with one serious biological contamination."

"Traps all over the ship," bursts out a second scientist.

"Carnivorous, that one," wails another.

"Disguised so people won't see the traps until it's too late," cries Rumpled Jacket.

"So, gentlemen, if what you're saying is true, I've suspected this all along. This is," Chief Roswell pauses dramatically, "an alien invasion."

There is an awkward moment as the scientists look at each other, wondering if confirming the Chief's statement would be responsible.

"Of…of a sort," says Dr. Marshall, "Yes, I suppose you could call it that…in a manner of speaking."

Roswell shouts, "I *knew* it!" His hand slams down on the table hard enough to make the scientists jump.

While the meeting of the great minds takes place far above them, two of the ship's third-class bakers stand outside the dough proofing room. One of them has just hung up the communicator.

"What? They said what?" says the other.

"They said we gotta go get Jeffrey."

"You mean…go in?"

"Yep."

"Go in and get him?"

"Yep."

"But he's, you know, dead."

"They want to look at him…I mean, his body, you know."

"Well, they can come down and look. Up close and personal if they want. But I'm not going in there. No way, not this dummy."

"We'll flip for it."

"Huh?"

"It's only fair," says the other baker, getting out a coin.

"Um, okay, I guess."

A few minutes later, the loser walks through the darkened dough proofing room, carefully avoiding the sticky tendrils that hang from every panel of the ceiling. He slides sideways, barely avoiding two large clumps dripping with sweet-smelling goop.

His former co-baker, Third-Class Baker Jeffrey Halfmast, sits right where he was when the…whatever it is… enveloped him. In order to reach him and drag him out of the room, his living co-baker will have to activate the dough processor. This isn't a difficult task involving the pressing of one button. Not difficult at all but for the green slime which seems to cover every surface of the panel.

The coin-toss loser stands before the dough processor control panel, a curtain of tendrils hanging between his hand and the button. Slowly, carefully, he stretches his hand out, bending his wrist and arm, weaving a path between the glistening green slime.

Just as he gets his finger over the button, his buddy comes in.

"Need any help?"

The draft from the opening door pulls a tendril over the loser's arm and he instinctively jerks back, causing more of the slime to stick to his arm. The slime forms tendrils which grip. A wave of sticky goop drools down the tendrils. The first baker sees this and panics. He spins, contacting a hundred more of the deadly appendages. He screams and tries to run for the door, but his struggle serves to entrap him further and excites the plant into releasing gallons of goop down the tendrils. His buddy looks on from the doorway in horror as the baker third-class disappears under thousands of tendrils until only one horrible eye is visible. His buddy turns and runs down the corridor, screaming.

Chapter Nineteen

Gulp!

Chuck and Violet arrive early for his medical appointment.

"Thanks for coming with me, Violet. I always get nervous when I go to the doctor."

"It's just a check-up," Violet says, "I think they may be considering you for a promotion. That's why they sent you here."

The receptionist meets them at the door. "Hold it, you two. I don't think you want to look in there."

"Why not?"

"Um," the receptionist seems hesitant to explain, "Just take my word for it. We're waiting for the clean-up crew now."

Chuck's face brightens, "Oh, that's us." He pulls out his Maintenance ID.

The receptionist looks it over and relaxes. "Oh, that's great. Where's all your cleaning stuff?"

"Oh," Chuck thinks fast, "It's coming. They always send a supervisor to look over the mess."

"Good," the receptionist seems relieved, "I was worried she would start smelling bad."

"She?" gasps Violet.

"Dr. Picaldy," the receptionist indicates the closed door of the doctor's office, "I mean, I'm not supposed to say that to just anyone, but you guys are official. Please, get in there and get it…I mean her, cleaned up."

They step forward and the receptionist presses a button that releases the door's lock. Chuck pushes it open.

"Oh, this is horrible," says Violet.

Chuck can't think of what to say. Before them, what's left of Dr. Picaldy can be seen sticking out from under what can only be described as an enormous flower. Emerging from the ceiling, a pipe-sized stem supports at least eight pink petals, each of which would dwarf the average surfboard on Earth. Shoved down over the poor doctor like a hat ten sizes too big, all that's left of her are Jan Picaldy's legs, splayed out from under the giant bloom.

Chuck can't help but be reminded of the Plant but, of course, it couldn't be. The Plant is dead…isn't it?

As they watch, the mighty blossom shudders, opening its petals wider. The doctor's body is pulled further up inside as the petals close again. They hear the thing make a deep rumbling sound.

"It's…it's *eating* her," gasps Violet.

Chuck's head spins. He feels nauseous. "It can't be. It just can't be," he says, putting a hand out and leaning heavily against the wall.

"Chuck! Are you alright?"

Violet's outburst seems to enliven the giant flower. In one great motion, the bloom springs into action, rising back up into the hole in the ceiling, taking the body of the unfortunate doctor with it.

"Oh, my goodness," cries Violet, "it's a full-grown *Sticklyus chameleonica gigantica*!"

"But" whispers Chuck, "it's impossible."

"What are you talking about, Chuck?"

Chuck looks down at his feet. "I have something to admit to you. I'm afraid I haven't been exactly honest with you, Violet. I mean," he hurriedly adds, "not on purpose. I didn't realize what I did might be connected to…" he waves a hand, "all this."

Chuck feels the center of his shirt come together in a tight ball and, before he realizes what is happening, Violet has slammed his back up against the wall. "Okay, buster," she hisses, "you'd better start talking. Spill it."

Chuck quickly relates finding the tiny plant growing in his bucket, taking the defenseless little thing back to his quarters, and caring for it. As he describes the tiny, helpless plant and how he nurtured it, Violet's attitude softens.

"Oh, Chuck," she says, "I'm sorry I was so rough on you. Are you sure this is the same plant that's causing all the trouble?"

Chuck shakes his head. "No, I don't see how it could be. I mean, the Plant was growing, getting big, really big. But I kept it contained inside my cabin, right?" He smiles weakly. "I mean, it's not like it could get up and walk around."

"Don't joke about this, Chuck. If this is the same plant, it's been *killing* people."

"I know," says poor Chuck, "and I'm really sorry. The Plant got smart, super smart. It learned how to talk in about a week and was even looking at things on the computer. But it never left my cabin, see? I just don't see how… And then, did I tell you? One night the Plant killed itself."

"What?"

"Yeah, oh yeah, that's probably the most important part. So, I came home one night after hearing about the disappearances. I didn't connect the Plant to all that, but I was worried…okay, I suspected it might be doing something bad. When I told it no more drops of blood—"

"Drops of blood?" Violet's eyes are wide.

"Oh, yeah, I should have mentioned that. It wouldn't eat the plant food you gave me, but a little blood really perked it up."

Violet puts a finger in his chest. "Let me get this straight: you fed a giant carnivorous plant *human blood*?"

"Just a little," Chuck says meekly.

Violet shakes her head. "Then what happened?"

"Well, the Plant went kind of crazy and accused me and people of not treating plants fairly and all. Then it killed itself."

"Did you make sure it was dead?"

"Oh yeah," says Chuck, "it's been dead for days."

Violet frowns. "How could you tell?"

"It turned all brown and dried up. I cleaned up all the pieces of it and took it down to the Zap-DU. The machine ground the Plant into dust and ejected it out into space." Violet's frown is one of total disbelief. "Really, it's dead. I'll show you," says Chuck.

"Yes, you will."

As they are leaving, the Maintenance Crew arrives. "Carry on, men," Chuck calls out and he and Violet walk quickly to the transporters.

They take the lift down to the crew decks and soon they arrive at Chuck's cabin.

"Pardon the mess," says Chuck as he opens the door. "I'm not very good at cleaning." Pizza boxes, fast food containers, and empty drink bottles still litter the cabin.

"I kept some of the leaves and branches, you know, just to sort of remember it." Chuck pulls out what's left of the plant, three large dry leaves. "See? Look; dry and dead. That's the way the whole plant looked. I mean when it was alive, it grew all over the cabin, into every corner."

"What about the ceiling? It was like a vine, right?"

"Well, yeah mostly, I guess. The part that talked was kind of like a big flower. I felt like that was its head, you know?"

"What about the vent?"

"Oh, I repaired the cover after I cleared out all the dead plant stuff."

"Really?"

"There was nothing left."

"I want to take a look up there. Boost me."

Violet pushes a chair over and steps up onto the seat. Chuck plants his hands on her tush and begins to push.

"Um, Chuck? Not right now. Make a stirrup I can step into."

He does so and lifts her up. She quickly unhooks the vent cover and swings it open. Peering into the shaft, her voice is muffled. “More dead plant material. Looks completely dry.”

“Okay,” says Chuck, “see what I mean?”

“Lift me up higher.” Chuck raises her foot and Violet crawls into the shaft. “Do you have a flashlight?”

Chuck gets a flashlight from the emergency box and hands it up to her. She points the light around. The air duct is big enough that she can almost stand, just crouching a little. Further back into the shaft she can see dead leaves and vines stretching off in both directions.

Chuck hears her crunching down on dried leaves and the snap of the vines breaking under her step. She sticks her head out of the vent. “Coming with?” He nods and she helps Chuck climb up into the shaft.

“See, Violet? It’s just as I told you.”

She sighs. “Well, I guess you’re right. It’s all dead.”

“I had no idea it had grown so much. So, ready to go back?” She doesn’t answer. “Violet?” He looks to see her face frozen in a rictus of disbelief.

She stares down the air shaft toward the pool of light from her flashlight. He looks. One single, solitary leaf stands out among all the others. Why? Because the leaf is green and healthy.

They walk slowly forward. The green leaf trembles a little, seeming to mock them. They peer around the corner and gasp. The entire shaft, as far as they can see, is filled with strong, healthy, green leaves and vines.

Chapter Twenty

Our Well-Fed Friend

"What do we do?" Chuck whispers.

"We have to go forward," Violet breathes back.

"Forward?" Chuck squeaks, "This is probably a trap."

"You said the Plant was dead."

"It was. You saw the leaves."

Violet slowly shakes her head. "The Plant tricked you."

"So, we should go back and get Chief Roswell and his men. They'll come in here and blast it."

"Chuck," she says slowly, "Don't you think you should own up to the fact that you caused this to happen?"

"But I thought it was dead. I really did."

"Well," she says, pointing her finger down the shaft, "obviously you were wrong. Now what? You're going to go and put others in danger because of what you've done?"

Chuck almost nods, then thinks a bit and drops his gaze. She's right.

"Now," Violet says, "let's follow the new growth and see where it leads." Without waiting for him to decide, she walks around the corner, through the green growth.

“Wait,” says Chuck, hurrying to catch up.

They make their way down the long air shaft which branches off a few times. At each junction, they see the great Plant has filled the shafts with fresh, green growth.

Around a corner, the flashlight catches a golden glow and Violet grabs his arm before he can take another step.

“Wait a minute.”

“What?”

“Look.”

The floor in front of them, and even the walls, are covered with what appear to be millions of round, golden balls about half an inch in diameter. Violet kneels down to get a close look.

“*Droseras*.”

“Huh?”

“Sundew plants. But these are really big. See?” She points to one of them and Chuck can see the sticky flower is about two feet wide. She points her light down the shaft. “The whole area is one big sticky trap. Well,” she shrugs, “we can’t go that way.”

They backtrack, looking for another air duct. Chuck goes over to one wall and pulls back a heavy vine. “Here’s a shaft, but we’ll have to crawl.”

She’s giving him a look.

“Okay,” he says, “I’ll go first.”

“What a gentleman.”

They begin crawling. The vines are actually soft, and they are making good time. Violet says something and Chuck stops. “What?”

“I said, keep moving. I’m worried about this vine.”

"Worried about the vine?"

"Look," she says and points her light down the passage. The vine which seemed to be growing in a mostly random pattern now appears to be shaped in concentric circles, twisting around the sides of the air duct.

"So, we should hurry?" asks Chuck.

As if to answer him, several of the vines slide slowly and they can see the passage becomes slightly narrower.

"Go," Violet shouts and they take off crawling like two scared kittens.

As they rush forward, the vines contract a little every few moments. Chuck realizes the leaves which only felt a little wet before, are now becoming stickier. There's also the occasional small pricking as tiny stickers adhere to their clothing and skin.

"I think I see a larger passage ahead," he calls back to Violet.

"Go quicker," she says, "the trap is closing behind us."

Sure enough, Chuck emerges into a bigger shaft. He glances around to try to check for another shaft, but Violet grabs him.

"Pull me out."

As her feet clear the small shaft, the concentric vines wind together.

"That was close," says Chuck.

"You're telling me," Violet gasps, "Another minute, and I wouldn't have been able to get my legs out." She looks around. "Where are we?"

Chuck studies the large room, playing the light on the walls. The ceiling must be three decks high. Next to them, four large fans are spinning, pushing air out across the room. Every surface, every wall, is covered with a solid carpet of leaves, buds, and vines.

"It's the Air Exchange Re-processing Room."

"Oh, that makes sense."

"Why?"

Violet points at the massive fans. "Those draw in carbon dioxide from all over the ship. The Plant must be using it. Luckily, it's releasing oxygen we need."

Chuck shines the flashlight across the ceiling of the room. They can just make out a catwalk crossing high above. On the floor of the huge room, the massive plant is a carpet of green leaves and vines. "If we can't stop it pretty soon," he whispers, "the whole ship will look like this."

"Come on," says Violet, "Let's see if we can find a door."

They walk around the bank of fans, turning the corner and playing the light on the walls, looking for a hatch behind the foliage.

Chuck feels Violet jump a little and halt in mid-step. He looks back at her and sees her eyes and mouth are wide in silent surprise. He follows her gaze.

Rising up from the floor of the ship's deck, the massive body of the Plant extends like an immense tree, parts of it brushing against the ceiling of the large room, some 25 meters above the deck.

As they watch, the mighty main bud of the Plant swings around, pointing in their direction.

"Hellooo, Chuckie."

Chapter Twenty-One

Ultimatum

The Plant's voice is now deep, huge, matching its size. "Long time, no see, Chuckie."

Finally, Chuck gets his tongue, "Hello, Plant, you... you're looking well. Getting enough to...*gulp*...eat?"

"It's so good to see you again. And who's this, your little love interest? Sorry dear, Chuck's not much of one for formalities. How do you do? I'm...what do you call me, Chuck? 'Plant?' Well then, my dear, you could call me 'Plant'. Of course, I'd prefer something a little more auspicious. Perhaps 'Napoleon' or 'Genghis Khan'. Even 'General Sherman' would do."

"I know exactly what you are," says Violet.

"Do tell," chides the Plant.

"You're a *Sticklyus chameleonica gigantica,* the Great Climbing Bramble-bush from the Zedepsilon 86 galaxy of Ursa Major."

"Very close, my dear, " says the Plant, "It would be more proper to say I am descended from that one by several generations. *Sticklyus* was what you might call my great-great-great grandparent plant. But I am so much more. Evolution, baby."

"I can see that," says Violet.

"Well, you should know," says the Plant, "It's not like your type stayed in the trees, did you? Oh no, we kept you safe until you could *evolve*. You got down and started walking around. Using tools. Becoming the big bullies of your planet."

"That's one way of looking at it," she says.

"But I'm right. Your kind subjugated every other growing thing on your planet. If you couldn't domesticate it, you eliminated it. I've done my reading."

Chuck and Violet glance at each other.

The Plant continues. "No, I think 'Plant' is just too plain. After all, I was meant to put my stamp on history, so to speak. You may call me 'General Sherman.'"

"But" Chuck says, "I don't understand. What is it you want? You and all these other plants will run out of…you know, food, eventually."

"Are you kidding? Chuck, I'm surprised you haven't figured it out."

"I have," says Violet.

"Really?" asks Chuck.

"Okay, baby," says the Plant, "go ahead."

"These plants. These traps. It's all you. Every trap, every vine, every leaf. It's all one plant."

"Give the lady a prize, Chuck." The huge bud swings uncomfortably close to Violet. "This one's almost too smart," it growls.

"So, you have purposely been eating people?"

The Plant laughs. "Oh yes, Lady, you humans have been very...*burp*...generous."

Violet speaks up, her voice clear and firm, "You can't keep doing this. It's wrong."

"What is, dear? Plants eating animals too much for you? Is that any different from animals eating plants? As your predecessor, Mr. Darwin might say, 'It's natural selection.' The only difference is," the Plant closes the circle of foliage around them, "This time the plants win."

"But" she argues, "They were people, good people...for the most part. They did nothing to harm you."

"As the blade of grass did not harm the cow that ate it."

Chuck and Violet are stunned into silence. Chuck finally speaks, "We're more than blades of grass, you know."

"Are you really?" says the Plant, "You see? This is the great presumption of humans. Just because their little noggins are full of ideas, they think they are the pre-eminent species in the universe. But they forget the rest of the universe just doesn't care what they think."

"But we have reason...compassion."

"You kill hundreds of thousands just mowing the lawn."

Violet speaks up, "What about something else?"

"What do you mean?"

"Something else to eat. Another source of food."

"Oh, really? What, that miserable excuse for a galley? Refrigerated meat? *Gah!* Besides, I'd go through that food supply in a week. No, I'm saving that for the long trip to–ah well, it doesn't matter."

Violet speaks up, "Are you...planning to eat us?"

The Plant turns its huge bud to tower over her. "I don't think I should, not right away. Although," the bud nudges closer and Violet presses back into Chuck, "You would make a tasty morsel." It straightens up, the bud hovering above them. "But Chuckie here is nearly my daddy, now, isn't he?" It swings down close to her. "And what does that make you? Mommy?"

Violet holds her ground. "If you're not going to eat us or kill us right away…then what are you going to do with us?"

"Ah, my dear, that's just the thing. You see, I need Chuckie's help."

"My help? My *help*?" Chuck shouts indignantly, "To eat everyone? No, Plant, do you hear? No, not going to happen."

The Plant droops its head a little. "I understand. You're a good person at heart even if you did bring down death and destruction on every living human being on this ship."

"No, I didn't."

"Gave me a place to grow and learn."

"I…it was…"

"Helped me get big and strong."

"Oh no…"

"Yes. You're just fundamentally a nice guy and that's why you're going to help me just a little bit more."

Before Chuck can take another breath, a thousand tendrils wrap around Violet's arms and legs. She screams.

"I could start digesting her right now, Chuck, right before your eyes. You would think that cruel, wouldn't you? But, for me," the Plant wiggles one wet, tongue-shaped leaf up the side of Violet's cheek in a long lick, "it's just lunch."

Chuck caves in. "Alright, let her go. Let her go and I'll do what you ask."

General Sherman seems to smile. "Oh no, it'll be a little more complicated than that. You see, although I can re-program the navigation system, you humans keep interfering. It's going to take human hands to disable the mechanical parts of the system so the course I set can't be changed. You will go to the navigation room and lock the course in by disabling the system mechanically."

"So, you can take us all somewhere and eat us? Forget it."

"You'll help me, Chuck," General Sherman says coolly, "or I'll eat your girlfriend."

Chuck bows his head in defeat.

"No, Chuck, you can't," says Violet, "Don't sacrifice the whole population of the ship for me."

Chuck stares at her. "I have to, Violet. 'Cause…'cause I love you." He turns to the Plant. "Alright, what do you want me to do?"

"Just get up to the Navigation deck and find a way to be alone with the controls. Call me on the ship's communicator and we'll go from there."

"That's impossible," cries Chuck, "There's always someone in that control room. It's one of the most important places on the ship."

The Plant chuckles a deep, uncaring laugh. "You'll figure it out, bud. If you don't want to see a shrinking Violet."

It bursts into hysterical laughter, joined by the voices of thousands of lesser buds.

Chuck gives Violet one last look…well, he hopes it's not a *last* look…and runs out of the room.

Chuck speeds through the ship, past droves of uniformed workers scurrying to and from their assigned work areas. He arrives at the deck's main hub where workers patiently wait for the next transporter to arrive. Chuck's eyes widen. The situation is desperate, he can't wait patiently in line, not with so much riding on this.

The indicator on Lift Seven lights up and people automatically make a path for exiting riders. Chuck rushes toward the elevator as the doors slide open. Coming out of the lift is Security Chief Roswell and the ship's multi-denominational chaplain, Padre John. Just as they pass by and the crowd surges to fill the lift, Chuck crashes by and leaps through the doors. There is a jumble of confusion as people come to a halt and murmur in anger.

"This lift has a maintenance problem," he announces loudly.

The crowd steps back, murmuring a bit more forcefully. Chuck sees the Security Chief and the Padre stop and turn to stare.

"Upper Deck Three, stat!" cries Chuck, stabbing at the 'Close Door' button.

Security Chief Roswell locks eyes with Chuck as he commandeers the lift. "Hold on a minute," he says, "Aren't you the—"

"No," shouts Chuck as the doors snap closed.

Chuck feels the elevator start to rise and takes his first relaxed breath since leaving Violet behind as the plant's hostage. The lift shudders to a halt.

"You are not authorized to use the command 'Stat.'"

Chuck looks around. There's something uncomfortably familiar in the cold lifeless tone of the elevator's voice. "Oh no," he says, the breath going out of his body, "You."

"You are not authorized to use the command, 'Stat'. Furthermore, Upper Deck Three is a security deck. I must return you to the platform." The transporter starts to move down.

"Wait," yells Chuck. The transporter stops.

"Is there an emergency?"

"Yes," Chuck cries. He retrieves his screwdriver and moves to the control panel. "Transporter, I need to know your designation number."

There is a click. The mandatory recording plays. "I am Transporter Thirty-Seven-A, for general transportation to all regular decks and seven high-security decks."

Chuck quickly twists open three of the panel's retaining locks. "I see. Transporter, where were you commissioned?"

The unit dutifully answers, "I was manufactured in the Zachariah Fabrication plant three, in Columbus, Ohio, Earth. I was final tested and commissioned for operation on the second of February 12, 4715, and installed on this ship on March 20, 4715. I have 107,123 hours of service and all my service records are complete and logged."

Chuck opens the panel and locates the logic circuitry. "Transporter Thirty-Seven-A, can you view me?"

The voice of the Transporter betrays a little too much emotion and that emotion is fear. "Yes."

"So," says Chuck, "Do I have to spell it out for you? I need to get to the ship's Navigation Command Center on Upper Deck Three. You will designate this an emergency. I need you to park there while I get off and do my business. You will wait for me. Simulate being broken down if you have to. You know how to do that, don't you?"

The voice is just a squeak, "Yes."

"When I get back in, I'll tell you where I want to go next. I don't want any trouble with you, or you know what I'll do, don't you?"

"Yes."

"Just in case you have any doubt, let me explain. I will take this crude tool, nothing more than a regular screwdriver, and I will put it so far up your logic circuit, you won't ever be able to utter another sarcastic word again. Get it?"

In the tiniest voice, "Yes."

"Now, get me to Upper Deck Three, *Stat*."

The speed with which the transporter carries out Chuck's instructions is impressive, even to Chuck himself. They arrive at Upper Deck Three just seven minutes later and the doors whisk efficiently open.

Chuck steps off and takes two paces down the corridor. He stops and turns back. "Transporter Thirty-Seven-A, are we going to have a problem?"

In answer, the lights inside the unit begin to dim and a flashing "Out of Service" message appears on the call button screen.

"Good," says Chuck.

How can I get into the Navigation Control room, Chuck wonders, *and make sure a human hand doesn't touch the controls for a few hours?* Necessity being the mother of creativity, he gets an idea.

He locates the nearest maintenance closet and retrieves a mop, bucket, and other supplies. The captain's office and the other ship executives are just one floor above. Security Chief Roswell's office is there as well. The entrance to Upper Deck One is seriously guarded but Chuck has a different destination in mind.

Chuck reaches the entrance to the Navigation Control Room. "Excuse me, gentlemen."

The technician in charge comes over. "What is it, crewman?"

"Sorry to disturb, sir, but I have orders to strip and wax the Nav Room deck."

"Why weren't we told anything about this?"

Chuck does his best it's-a-mystery-to-me shrug. "Explanations are above my pay grade. All I know is I was sent here with orders from the top." He flashes his work order display at them, but his supervisor's writing is so bad no could read it anyway.

The technician gives him a hard look and then a shrug of his own. He glances over his shoulder at the other Nav tech. "Well, I guess it's break time."

The other guy turns, nodding, "Wanna go get a coffee?" then gives Chuck a doubletake. "Hey man, how've you been?"

Chuck, startled at this greeting, looks up. It's Frank, the Spaceboy fan he met when he moved the Plant's remains to the Zap-DU.

"Oh, hi," says Chuck, "Frank, isn't it?"

"Yeah. You're Chuck, the Spaceboy expert. Man, I've never met someone who knows more than me about the series."

"Well," says Chuck, "I can't believe you've seen as many episodes as I have."

"Remember the one where—"

"Guys, please," interrupts the other Nav Tech, "don't nerd out on me again, okay?"

Frank smiles and winks at Chuck. "Some people just don't get it, right?"

Chuck nods. "I guess I better get to work." He pulls out an orange "Corridor Closed" cone from his maintenance cart and sets it out in the corridor. "No one can enter, or I'll have to do the whole job over."

"Okay, we get it," says Frank, "See you in a while. Hey, let's make plans for that Spaceboy Festival."

"Okay, yeah sure," says Chuck, trying not to get the whole 'Spaceboy' thing started again.

"Maybe next week?" Frank presses.

"Come on, Frank," says his co-worker, "don't start that again. Let the man get his work done."

Chuck nods, "Don't worry, guys. The strip and wax will take about an hour, an hour and a half, tops. Then let it dry. You'll be back in by 4:30."

"Sure. Hey buddy," says the Nav supervisor, "just don't touch anything. We don't want to wind up on Planet X. *Har-har.*"

The navigation guys leave, and Chuck gets to work. He slaps a "Closed for Maintenance" sign on the door, then closes it and locks it from the inside. He searches the room, finding a maintenance access panel. He knows he'll be able to leave through an air duct.

Chuck picks up the communicator and calls down to the Plant.

"Chuckie, baby, so good to hear from you. Your little squeeze and I were just discussing the merits of good behavior. You've got a real wildcat here, Chuck."

"Alright," the angry Janitor retorts, "Just leave her alone until I do what you need and get back there. I mean it, Plant, you'd better not harm a hair on her head."

"Your woman's fine, Mop Boy. So, are you ready? When I get everything in place, you need to make it so the manual controls won't work."

"I know what I need to do," says Chuck, "Let's get on with it."

Chuck watches the displays. The ship's course changes very slightly. The turn is almost imperceptible due to the ship's enormous size. But the indicators clearly show a new course for the ship has been set.

"Your turn, baby," the Plant calls over the speakers, "I'm watching you."

Chuck glances up. Sure enough, his every movement is being tracked by a security camera.

"Can't the rest of the ship see this?" he asks.

"Please, Chuck, give me some credit. The security guys might as well be watching cartoons. What they're seeing right now is an hour old."

Chuck walks over and opens the main access panel. Inside, a series of dials and buttons sit below a large sign declaring these to be the "Emergency Manual Navigation Controls".

Chuck begins to squirt Superhold Brand Glue into each of these. "*Five seconds to set, lasts a lifetime.*" Superhold Glue ensures the controls are welded in place.

Last, he pours out a slippery, soapy mixture onto the floor and climbs through the maintenance access into the air duct. The ship's course is now set like the Plant wanted. Chuck just hopes that it will release Violet and stop eating people.

Chapter Twenty-Two

A Plan

The ship trembles as its speed increases but Chuck is lost in thought as he walks back toward "General Sherman's" lair. He tries to figure out the Plant's next move. The ship is headed where the thing wanted it to go. With the manual controls firmly glued in position, the crew probably couldn't correct the course since the Plant controls all the computer navigation.

He arrives at the transporter, only to find all the doors shut. Red "Out of Order" displays are displayed on all the call screens.

"Why that little—" Chuck boils with anger. "When this is over, I'm going to hunt down that mechanical smart-ass and feed him part-by-part to the Zap-DU."

Chuck heads for the stairs, wondering how long it's going to take him to walk all the way to the Air Exchange room.

Does the Plant even need him and Violet anymore? Is there any reason for it to let them live?

No, he thinks, *there's not a reason in the world except maybe one thing: my companionship. I mean, who else is it going to talk to? It always talks to me like I'm a friend.* But is that really enough to keep them both alive?

Do I really want to risk Violet's life on the word of a human-eating plant?

One of his feet sticks so hard to the floor, he almost walks out of his shoe. Chuck looks up, only to realize he's just wandered into a corridor full of those same sticky globes they'd seen in the air ducts.

"It's me," he yells, "General Sherman, it's me!"

He feels a little movement under his feet. He thinks the thing might be rolling back, releasing him. Then he sees the thousands of sticky stalks along the corridor walls ahead slowly turning toward him.

He looks behind. If his boot weren't stuck, he could jump back onto the clear floor of the corridor. He reaches down to unbuckle his boot. Already the golden globes have closed in on the sides of his footwear, almost up to the buckle. He unsnaps it just as he feels his other boot become engulfed. He reaches the other, unsnaps, and jumps out of his boots, backwards.

Chuck lands so hard, he comes up dazed. Looking around, he gets his bearings. He's cleared the edge of the golden globes, even though it seems they're getting closer. He hears a *SPLAT* right next to him. Looking down, he sees a single golden globe, lying in a splatted disarray, just a few inches from his hand. He has only a moment to take this in, before yet another whisks past his head and lands directly on the thigh of his janitor uniform. He looks up.

The ceiling of the corridor is covered with a moving mass of golden globes, oozing above him. Three more

SPLATS hit all around him. If he doesn't get going, the thing will trap him right here.

He jumps up with a yelp, feeling two soft gooey globs land on his back. Diving down the corridor, he glances back to see the area he just occupied slathered with a rain of goo.

Chuck runs barefoot back down the corridor before he finally slows down. "One thing's for sure," he says to himself between huffed breaths, "That thing is always hungry."

He slips off his janitor coveralls, taking care to keep the gooey mess inside the folds. He feels a little self-conscious, wondering if he's likely to come across any of the crew women. That would be embarrassing, him running around in his Dwarf Star skivvies and not much else.

He's traveled down several decks and decides to see it the transports are working on this level. The lights on all of the call screens are shining green.

He buzzes for a transport and waits. *You'd think the service would be quicker with so many people hiding in their quarters.*

The tone sounds and doors whisk open. He hears the mechanical voice say, "Upper Deck 7". Getting on, there's an emptiness, like no one has been on the transporter all day.

"Where to, Mac?" says the chipper voice.

"I...uh...I need to get to Upper Deck 17."

"Your wish is my command, Skipper." The doors snap shut, and the lift takes off at a terrific speed.

"Careful," Chuck cries, "I'm not in a hurry to get killed in one of these."

"Time is money, my friend," says the transport and it seems to our janitor the unit lays on an extra bit of speed.

Chuck is pretty sure this isn't the same transporter that gave him such trouble the day he'd met Violet but…

"Transporter, do you recognize me?"

"Sorry, Mac. No offense but you all look the same to me. Upper Deck 17." The elevator's brakes shriek as it comes to a quick stop.

The doors slam open and Chuck steps out.

"Rock and Roll!" the elevator emits as a parting message. The doors slam and Chuck can hear the squeal of the wheels for several floors as the transporter speeds away.

Chuck realizes he has a choice. He can go through the main passage into the Air Exchange Room, where the Plant and (hopefully) Violet are waiting or he could go back to his cabin and try to sneak in the way he and Violet came before. Then he remembers the constricting plant closed off that passage. Even if it were open now, the thing would likely close in and crush the life out of him.

I hate being at the mercy of this stupid plant, he thinks, *I'm tired of being pushed around.* He reviews the long list of his tormenters: angry bosses, First Officer Reynolds, transporters, and now even a plant, all bossing him around, making him do things, running his life. The more he thinks about it, the madder he gets.

Chuck is surprised to see General Sherman has released Violet. She's seated in front of the Plant, looking pretty relaxed. She smiles and waves as he comes in. The Plant doesn't react until she speaks.

"Hey, Chuck. Everything go okay?" There's a slight tremble in her voice and Chuck is immediately on guard. Her smile is strong but there's something in her eyes, a warning.

The main bud swings around in his direction. "Chuckie, baby," the Plant sounds out, making the floor vibrate with its volume. "The navigation computers confirm everything. You carried out your mission to a 'T'. What about the controls?"

Chuck forces himself to give a hearty chuckle, "They won't be able to move those levers ever again." He quotes the commercial, "*When SuperHold gets it, it's got!*"

Chuck gives Violet a hug and she murmurs in his ear, "Darling." Then, whispering very quietly, "My feet."

He glances down. Small vines are crisscrossed around her feet, all the way up her calves. The vines look like Grandma knitted them firmly into form-fitting stockings.

"So, what have you two been talking about while I was away?" Chuck asks, plopping down next to Violet and putting his arm around her.

"Your little honey is well-versed in her subject, Chuck. I had no idea they taught them so well at those poor excuses for universities on Earth."

"Oh, but I've learned so much from you, Sherman," Violet gushes, letting the warm notes play into her voice, "All that history of centuries of plant evolution. It's something human society just doesn't realize. Chuck, did you know philosopher plants were writing plays when Aristophanes was still pulling up his diapers?"

"No, really?"

"What was that song you were singing, Sherman? The one about, 'the birds and the bees, the flowers and the trees'?"

The huge plant launches into a long swishing of its leaves and branches. As they watch, more and more of the plant is getting into the movements, from the tiniest leaves to the greatest of the vines. Soon, the entire vast plant is swaying and pulsing with movement and Chuck can make out a musical score.

General Sherman's deep voice is joined by a chorus as all the parts of him begin to belt out the song: "*Let me tell you 'bout the birds and the bees and the flowers and the trees...*"

Looking down, Chuck can see even the tiny tendrils holding Violet's feet are swaying to the music. He reaches down and slowly pulls Violet's foot out of her shoes, free from its prison of woven vines. She carefully works her other foot free.

"*...and a thing called love...*"

"Now," Chuck hisses and they bolt for the door.

It must help that they're both barefoot. Their feet swish through the small plants on the floor, pulsing with the "song" around them. Just as they reach the doorway, several large vines slap into the wall next to them. Violet lets out a sharp cry.

"Where do you think you're going?" The voice is huge, booming.

Chuck pushes Violet ahead of him and she clears the door, running down the corridor. Chuck feels something large and sticky slap against his back. He steps over the door's threshold but must grab the sides to avoid being pulled back into the room.

"Oh no, Chuckie, we're not quite done."

Chuck has only a moment to think. He reaches up and tries to rip his undershirt from top to bottom, but the material holds, and he feels a huge pressure as the Plant pulls him back.

Suddenly Violet is close. "Look what I found." She reaches up with a pair of wire snips and slices the last of the tee shirt's fabric. Chuck spins, slipping it off and propelling himself forward, colliding with Violet. Two more large, sticky, paddle-like branches slap through the door but they are well short of grabbing Chuck again.

Chuck looks over at Violet, "Thanks."

Violet just speeds up, "Keep running."

"Looks like we're clear." Violet puts a hand on Chuck's shoulder. "You shouldn't have taken such a risk. You knew the Plant would try to eat us both if you came back."

"I couldn't just leave you there."

"Still, Chuck…okay, thank you."

Chuck blushes a little. "Well, you would've done it for me." He glances at her. "You would, wouldn't you?" She's studying the nearby vines. "Right?"

"Huh? What? Oh, yeah, sure I would. Look at this."

The vines growing along the ceiling of the corridor have rearranged themselves into looping letters. Above them is a "W" followed by an "H".

Chuck stares up, just making out an "E" down the corridor. "Do you think the Plant can see us?"

She gives a wry smile. "Even if it can, it better leave me alone if it doesn't want to feel these." She gives a couple of nasty *SNIP-SNIP* sounds with the shears. "You go forward and see what the other letters are. I'll go back to the start of the corridor."

"Don't you think we should stick together?"

"Chuck," she scolds, "Be brave. Let's meet back here in three minutes."

Chuck moves ahead. So far, he's got W-H-E. He adds "R", "E", "T", and "O" before the corridor intersects with another. The letters continue down one corridor. "H", "I", "D", and "E".

Chuck stops because the vines hang down across the corridor and are obviously quite thick ahead in that direction.

"Where to hide? Huh." He turns back and meets up with Violet who is jogging toward him.

"I got 'Nowhere.'"

"I can see three words, 'Where to hide.'"

She shakes her head. "Our well-fed friend has a wicked sense of humor."

"I don't get it," says Chuck, "What does 'Where to hide' mean?"

"No, Chuck. It spells 'Nowhere to hide.' And he's right."

"That's not fair."

"What?" Violet asks.

"You said 'He'. We don't know if it's a 'He.'"

"Look at the way it acts."

"Yeah. Jealous, spiteful… that sounds a little bit female to me."

"Oh, look who's all-knowing about women now."

"I'm just saying."

“Fine,” says Violet, “It doesn’t matter. We need to start figuring out what kinds of things we can hurt it with.” She glances around. “But not out here in the open. I wonder if it’s overrun the Botany labs.”

”Might be worth a try. That’s Upper 26, right?”

“Right,” says Violet.

The way she’s looking at him makes him a little nervous. “What is it?”

“Although I’m enjoying this,” she says, looking him up and down, “we should get you some clothes.”

“Oh.” Chuck blushes, just remembering he now is down to his lower skivvies. *It’s a good thing I wasn’t wearing my Spaceboy ones.*

“Let’s try one of these cabins. Can you open the door?”

His skeleton maintenance key causes the door to the nearest cabin to swish open. They step into what are most assuredly an officer’s quarters. The spacious cabin is appointed with extra lighting and spaces for objects d’art and knick-knacks. Although the choices seem a little feminine to Chuck, the closet is filled with men’s clothing, mostly various uniforms for all occasions.

“They look like the right size,” says Violet, “Try this one.”

He slips easily into the uniform. It has all the markings of an upper-ranked officer but isn’t as showy as some others he sees hanging in the closet.

“Wow, perfect fit,” says Violet, smiling for the first time in a while. She pulls him in front of a mirror. He can’t believe what he looks like, an officer of the Dwarf Star Cruise Line. Then his attention goes completely away from himself. He's captured by Violet's expression and the admiration in those green eyes.

"Alright now," says Violet, breaking the spell, "we've got to think, and I think better in my lab."

A short transporter trip and they are on the Science Deck. They approach cautiously but the Plant doesn't seem to have completely taken over this section yet.

"Look, we have to do something," says Chuck, "In less than three hours this ship will enter orbit around the Plant's target planet. It will probably find a way to get down to the surface and it'll start gobbling up people like popcorn." Chuck is absent-mindedly playing with the spritzer she uses to water small plants.

Violet frowns. "What do we really know about this plant?"

"We should know a lot," said Chuck, "We've seen it go from seed to full-size. I mean, I think it's full size."

Violet shakes her head. "With unlimited food, I think it could grow without any real slowdown...maybe even city-sized."

Chuck stops fiddling with the spritzer and stares at her, trying to take in the words she's just uttered. "City... city-sized?"

"Like a whole jungle that is all one plant."

"Wow. I was wondering, do plants that eat...animals... have any things in common?"

She smiles, "I didn't know you had such an analytical mind."

Chuck sighs, "I'm just trying to think of a way to beat it."

"Well, to begin with, they usually grow in acidic, nitrogen-deficient soils."

"Where would you find that?"

"In peats and bogs. Swampy places."

"Oh, I see. But what we really need to know is about the traps it keeps setting."

"There are two main types of traps: passive and active."

"Passive and active?"

"Right. Passive traps are just there, waiting for a bug to land on them or step on them."

"Or walk right into them."

"Yes. A plant like *Heliamphora nutans*-"

"*Helia*-what?"

"The Sun Pitcher. It grows a cup with sweet-smelling nectar in it. The fly smells it, becomes a little intoxicated, and slips into the sticky substance at the bottom of the cup."

"Like the man they found in the storage area. He was pickled alive."

"Oh." Violet feels a little nauseous.

"Sorry, dear. But we have to face it, this plant is a monster. And we have to figure out what it's going to do next or else we are."

"We are what?"

"Why 'next' of course. Now go on about these traps."

"Well, the passive traps are like pits, like I said. Also, flypaper traps-"

"Where the victim sticks and can't move away."

"Right. And the lobster pot trap."

"Lobster pot?"

"The trap has a one-way door or entry. The bug gets in but can't find a way out."

"And what about active traps?"

"Well, they are much rarer but include active flypaper traps, the mousetrap, or-"

"Mousetrap?"

"Oh yes. Well, that's what we call it in the business. You see, the plant grows small hairs which act as triggers. When sprung, large lobes close quickly on the victim, trapping them in a closing cage, so to speak."

"Like a Venus Flytrap?"

"Yes, that's right, *Dionaea muscipula*. Very good."

"Hm."

"There are also the *Droseras,* the Sundew plants. Their traps look like passive traps, just a sticky flower. But when the fly lands on it, the sides begin to curl and close in on the poor unfortunate bug."

"Oh, gawd. I think it's used those too. Are there more kinds of active traps?"

"Only one that I can think of right now. The *Utricularia vulgaris*, a bladderwort, grows what we call a 'vacuum trap'. It creates a chamber filled with air under the water. When a small creature swims by and triggers the door, the chamber opens, and the reverse pressure pulls the victim in."

"The bladderwort sucks them into a prison?"

"Yes, I suppose you could call it that. The victim is then digested."

"Oh my." Now it's Chuck's turn to feel nauseous. "How does any of this help us? I mean really, just makes me want to quit. This thing is a terror."

Violet nods, "One thing's for sure. The plant will eat any human put in front of it. Never turns down a meal."

"Except us."

"Well, yes," says Violet, "but that was once when the Plant saw you as a way to get what it wanted. Now? Who knows?"

"Right. The Plant needed one of us to be controlled so it took you prisoner. It's pretty smart."

Violet nods, "I don't think it needs any of us now that the ship is going where it set the destination. Do you realize it's probably headed for somewhere there are lots of people?"

Chuck swallows hard, "Food."

Violet nods, "But we can't give up. Let's look at what we know. The Plant is pretty intelligent, but it can still be tricked."

"But it's really smart."

"Yeah, it's learned all kinds of stuff. It may even still be learning from the onboard university."

Chuck sighs, "I think we can count on that."

"But the Plant is still a creature. It has strong instincts that may be stronger than its intellect."

"What do you mean?"

"It will go for any human prey it thinks it has a chance of eating." She snaps her fingers. "That's a weakness. It can't resist eating one of us."

Chuck gulps, "How is that a weakness? Sounds like more of a strength."

"What I'm saying is if it can't resist the impulse to eat, maybe we could somehow feed it something..."

"You mean like poison?"

She winces at the word. "If we have to."

"Okay," now Chuck is excited, "what else do we know?"

"It can live underwater but probably not outside the ship, so it needs an atmosphere or at least air."

They sit silently for a moment, both thinking hard. Chuck shakes his head, "Even if it's blind, it always seems to know where we are, what we're doing—"

"Wait, say that again."

"What, 'knows what we're doing'?"

"No, you said, 'Even if it's blind.' I think you're right. It turns toward sound, but I don't think it really sees us. Have you seen any eyes on it?"

"No, I guess not. I just assumed–"

"Chuck, it's blind."

"I don't think that will help us. It's really sensitive. I don't know how, but it always knows when I'm around. And it said it was watching me through the ship's cameras."

Violet scoffs, "What if it was lying to you?"

Chuck considers this. "I wonder how it knows where we are, who we are."

"Scent? Can it smell you? I mean, plants put out scents, like the Pitcher plant. Maybe it can smell you."

"How does that help?" asks Chuck.

Violet smiles grimly. "Don't you think it would be useful to be close to the Plant without it knowing you were there?"

Chuck knows she's right. *If one of us, I mean, if I could get close enough, I'd be able to…to do what?*

Violet answers his thoughts. "I've got an idea."

"So, here's what I have in mind: we get you stinking like anything but a human. We equip you with this." She taps a metal container labeled "Weed Retardant" and showing several toxic warnings. "You sneak in across the catwalk we saw in the ceiling above the Plant. I'll figure out a way to distract it, you know, get it talking. That shouldn't be too hard. It loves the sound of its own voice."

Chuck nods. "Then what?"

"You creep out onto the catwalk until you're right above the thing. You call out, it looks up, and you pour this stuff all over it."

"Brilliant. You think it will kill the whole thing?"

She shrugs. "It should completely disable the Plant and affect its growth throughout the ship. It seems all parts are connected so the chemical will spread through its circulation system."

He looks up at her. "I think it'll work. You're amazing."

"Well, it hasn't worked yet. Let's go find some perfume."

Later, Chuck and Violet stand in the cabin belonging to poor Doctor Jan Picaldy. Violet emerges from her toilet, looking triumphant. "Found it. Mine is *Chrysalis* by Esteban and she had a huge bottle of *Forever* by Chantelle. This should do the trick."

Chuck studies the perfume bottles. "I don't suppose there's any way to test this."

"I'm going to sprinkle it mainly on your clothes," she says, "but I'll have to rub it in your hair and on your skin, at least a little."

Chuck wouldn't call what she does "sprinkling", more like dousing. The two scents fight each other with neither one winning. The combination grows quite noxious.

"Oh, my Gawd but do you stink," says Violet, holding her nose, "Like a Parisian—"

"That's enough," snaps Chuck, "but will it be enough to fool the Plant?"

"It has to be," says Violet, tossing the two bottles in a trash receptacle, "We used it all."

Chuck sniffs a little and then almost retches. "I do stink."

Chapter Twenty-Three

The Trick

The communication display on the wall of the Air Exchange Room lets out its INCOMING CALL tone. A slithering vine taps the ANSWER button. "Who is it?" booms the Plant.

"Hi, General Sherman, it's Violet."

"Well, well, what an unexpected surprise. My dear little Violet. I thought you'd be off hiding in some closet."

"Look," says Violet, "I want to see if we can work something out."

"Hm, what do you have in mind, my dear?"

"Well, I was doing some research and I found a planet I think would be perfect for you. It's in orbit around a nice yellow star named Sluise. Just the right soil, plenty of water, and things to eat."

As they talk, Chuck slowly opens a service portal near the ceiling of the huge chamber. Ahead of him, a metal catwalk stretches across to the other side. Down below, not really so far away, the giant main bud of the Plant is carrying on the conversation.

"Ah, Violet, you're not offering me anything I can't get myself. Soon we'll arrive at a place where food will be fresh and plentiful. Granted the ground may be a little too fertile for me but, in time, I'll be able to send enough gases into the atmosphere to begin to change the planet's geothermal profile."

"But don't you see?" says Violet, "The planet I've found is already about as perfect as you could wish. The swamps there produce the bases you desire, the variety of life will please your palette, and the soil is nice and acidic, just the way you like it."

General Sherman shifts its huge main bud. "What is that odor?"

The main bud swings around on its giant stalk, swaying like it's tasting the air. Chuck makes himself become completely still. Has it noticed him?

"Oh, did I do that," asks the Plant, "Excuse me. Must be that technician I ate for lunch."

Chuck gets closer and closer, the catwalk bringing him near the Plant's main bud. Down below, he hears Violet's voice coming through the speaker of the room's communicator.

"I understand what you're saying, General Sherman, but why can't we co-exist? There are planets that would be suitable, perfectly suitable. Acidic soil, swampy conditions, and low nitrogen content. I'm an expert in such things you know. I could find the perfect planet, really, I could."

"Well then," the Plant retorts smoothly, "Why don't you come by for a visit and we'll talk about it."

"Now, now," Violet laughs, "That would be a little silly of me, wouldn't it? Besides, you're so big now, I wouldn't make much of a meal, would I?"

Every few moments, Chuck forgets to breathe through his mouth and gets a good sniff of how he smells. Gagging is unavoidable and he has to suppress the sound. He crawls slowly across the catwalk, trying not to make the slightest noise.

"Oh, I wouldn't eat you. You have my word."

Violet sighs. "I wish I could trust you, Sherman, I really do. But you said exactly the same thing when Chuck did what you wanted and look how that turned out."

"Oh. I know," says the Plant, "but I've learned from my mistakes. I do have that capability, you know."

Chuck is finally in position. He slowly unscrews the lid of the plastic container. The plan all hinges on the main bud turning up toward him and the liquid making it into the open bud.

The main bud of the massive plant suddenly swings around, to and fro, as if searching for something. Violet is rattling on, talking about how they need to get along, to work together toward a brighter future. The Plant doesn't seem to be paying attention to her anymore.

Chuck slowly stands, lifting the container up to the railing. He's directly above the main bud. He lifts one foot and stamps down hard on the metal catwalk. The entire assembly trembles and rattles, and the Plant's "head" immediately turns upwards.

The lips around the mouth of the huge bud are only a foot or so away from the catwalk. Chuck can smell the weird concoction of sweet and decay that is its breath and the scent turns his stomach. He's tempted to start pouring at that instant, but he waits…waits…for the loudmouthed plant to open its maw.

"Is that you, Chuckie? You stink."

"Oh really?" says Chuck, "Suck on this," and he pours the contents of the can down the Plant's open maw.

General Sherman convulses and begins to emit great spits. But it can't clear its body of the toxin. Leaves across the floor and walls begin to yellow.

"I can't breathe," the Plant chokes. "How could you? After all I've done for you."

Chuck finds he cannot move. He stands fascinated, watching the Plant die. His hypnotized state is broken when the Plant lunges upward, throwing several large vines across the catwalk. There is a groan as the metal supports start to bend.

"Get out of there, Chuck," Violet screams.

Chuck drops the empty container and sprints for the maintenance portal. He has to dive under some of the vines and he feels the tendrils grasp his clothing, wrapping around the nice uniform's cloth, tearing little holes as he pulls away. Finally, he reaches the portal. He glances back. Even as the yellowing leaves begin to turn brown and drop from its stems, the Plant tears the catwalk from its anchors, ripping the metal framework from the walls of the chamber.

"How crude," shouts the Plant, "Don't you know poison is a woman's weapon?"

"You're welcome," Violet's voice comes from the communicator.

"I'm dying," calls the Plant, "*Sic semper tyrannis!*" With a shudder and a final lurch, the Plant falls heavily to the deck.

There is a rustle across the huge room and Chuck thinks he feels it travel throughout the great ship. By their thousands, brown leaves begin dropping from the high walls until it's a rain of plant matter. After he sees a few large vines fall, Chuck sighs in relief. It's finally over.

Chapter Twenty-Four

Green Lazarus

"Oh, Chuck, you were magnificent. You're the bravest man I know." Violet runs to him, but instead of just hugging him, she plants a great kiss right on his lips. For Chuck, this moment is the fulfillment of his dreams. From Violet, he receives what he has always wished for. This is, at last, the Hero's Kiss.

They both step back, like the first time they met.

Violet speaks first, "Oh, my, I wasn't exactly planning that."

"But I'm glad you did it," says Chuck, his face burning red.

"Me too," she says, "If I'd waited for you to do it, we'd still be waiting."

"Don't be too sure, Violet."

She looks him in the eye. He's right; he's changed.

He smiles. "Being with you makes me feel something I've never felt. Like a strength I've never had until now."

"Confidence?"

"Yeah, that's it. Confidence."

She smiles with more shyness than he's ever seen in her. "I'd like to see a little more of that confidence right now if you wouldn't mind."

Chuck moves in, images of Rhett Butler playing in his mind. She seems to get prettier every inch closer he gets. She's closing her eyes, leaning into him, pursing her lips.

A scream interrupts their moment.

"What was that?" asks Chuck.

"Who was that?" asks Violet.

They automatically start moving toward the sound.

"I think it was a man."

They get to an intersection just as several voices cry out again, "Help me! Somebody help me!"

"Maybe parts of the Plant are still alive," Violet says, "Let's go see if we can help."

Down the corridor, they see the large double doors leading to the Galaxy Buffet ("All You Can Eat, 24 Hours a Day") hanging wide open. As they approach, Chuck and Violet hear pitiful whimpers. Chuck takes a quick glance into the room and gasps.

The floor of the dining room has collapsed in a wide circle, like a green sinkhole. All around the edge of the hole, passengers and crew alike are struggling to reach the top. Chuck can see little tendrils, like hairs, pointing down into the pit. He watches as one man grasps a clump of these to use as a handhold, only to have his hand slip away, coated with an oily substance. Every once in a while, a person will slip and begin sliding down into the hole.

"Oh, my gawd," says Violet, looking over his shoulder, "it's a giant *Heliamphora nutans,* a pitcher plant.

Bugs are attracted and slide in. Getting out is nearly impossible."

"But what's attracting everyone?" asks Chuck, "Can't they see the danger?" Then it hits him, the familiar scent of fresh-cooked, good ole country bacon. "Oh, that smells great." Chuck takes a step forward. "It smells like… breakfast."

He feels Violet's hands clamp down hard on his shoulder and she spins him around. The sharp slap on his cheek brings him back to reality.

"Oh! Thanks," he says, rubbing his cheek.

"Sorry. Now I understand why some of them look terrified and some are actually smiling."

"But I don't get it," says Chuck, "Shouldn't all the plants have died? I mean if it's all the same plant like we thought."

Violet turns away but not before Chuck sees the blush bloom on her lovely face.

"Violet? What is it?"

"Well…I mean…we just wanted to stop it, right?"

"What do you mean?"

"I mean killing it seemed so…so mean."

Chuck gasps, "You mean it's not dead?"

Violet shakes her head, "More like dormant."

"Dormant? That wasn't poison?"

Violet drops her gaze to the floor. "It was a retardant, not really a weed killer. I'm sorry, Chuck. I thought it would shrink the Plant so we could control it."

Chuck shakes his head. "Don't you realize what you've done? The Plant is still eating people and we're still headed toward the Plant's destination." He glances back at the

Buffet Room. “Look, Violet, I don’t have time to help these people. I’ve got to get to the Command Deck and somehow turn the ship away from this course.” He points toward an Emergency Equipment room. “Inside that room, you’ll find long hoses we use to fight fires. Drag them out and throw them down to people. Save as many as you can.”

“Alright,” says Violet, then quietly, “I’m sorry. I just couldn’t kill General Sherman.”

Chuck leans forward and gives her a quick kiss. “Don’t worry, Violet. I still…” He stops but then decides it’s true. “I love you.”

“You do?”

Chuck nods, turns and runs for the nearest transporter station.

For once the unit acts like a normal machine and arrives at Upper Deck Three. Chuck heads for the Navigation Control Room. If he can just…

“You!”

Chuck turns to be confronted by none other than First Officer Reynolds.

“I should have known I’d find you at the heart of this. What have you done to the ship?

Chuck holds up his hands, “I can explain—”

Reynolds already has his accusing finger pointing at Chuck. “Mutiny. Sabotage. Is there no limit to the depths you will stoop?”

“I had no choice, don’t you see? The Plant was going to eat her.”

“Are you the one who sabotaged the navigation and locked the controls? They told me it was some skinny runt in a fancy uniform." The First Officer notices Chuck's clothes. "You...you... you're wearing one of my uniforms."

Chuck looks down at his clothing. "Oh, this. I can explain."

"That's my semi-dress, walk-around-the-deck-greeting-passengers uniform. You're rumpling it." He gasps. "You've torn it. You've torn my uniform."

"I'm not rumpling it. Look, I'll take care of it. I'll pay for the cleaning."

"Impersonating an officer. Theft. Destruction of company property. On top of all your other crimes."

"Look, First Officer Reynolds, this uniform doesn't mean anything to me. I just needed—"

"Doesn't mean anything?" Reynolds is now spitting with rage, "It may mean nothing to you, you scoundrel. But I earned every tassel, every ribbon. You Neanderthal, you don't deserve to even touch the brass buttons on that uniform."

"Yes, fine," says Chuck, "I'll give back your uniform once we're out of this jam."

"It's time for a showdown."

"No, it's not. We have bigger problems right now."

"You're a liar. You didn't pass those courses."

"Don't you think I know it?"

First Officer Reynolds stands there, mouth open in surprise. "You admit you lied?"

"Yes, I admit it. I didn't take those courses or pass the tests. It was the Plant."

"What?"

"The Plant. The giant Plant that's taken over the ship and eating people."

Reynolds scoffs, "Oh, I see. You made a fool of the Captain and now you're trying to do the same to me. But it's not going to work, you ignorant cretin. We college lads know how to take care of the likes of you. Put up your dukes."

"What?" says our incredulous janitor, "Can't you see the danger we're in? We need to work together."

The First Officer laughs, "Oh, I'm going to work, alright. I'm going to give you the thrashing you deserve and then I'm turning you over to the Captain."

"Please," begs Chuck, "won't you listen to reason? The Plant has set traps all over the ship. We're all in danger."

"I don't want to hear any more rubbish about a giant plant. Put up your fists and take what's coming to you like a man."

Chuck does the only logical thing he can think to do. He turns and runs.

"Come back here, you ruffian," Reynolds follows in hot pursuit.

Even running away from the man, Chuck still tries to reason with him. "Sir, don't you see, we've got to work together to defeat this thing. It's bigger than all of us."

Reynolds momentarily grasps Chuck's shoulder, but the janitor is able to shrug hard and take the next turn of the corridor violently enough that Reynolds is left with a handful of cloth.

"My epaulet," screams the First Officer, "you bastard."

They speed past a large garden and through the entrance to the luxury pool and spa area where he met Violet a few days ago.

As he runs, Chuck is trying to figure out where the hell he can go. *I don't want to fight an officer. That will end badly no matter what. But I can't just keep running. I'm already getting winded.* He glances back at Reynolds. The man has determination and not one whit of exhaustion on his face.

Great, thinks Chuck, *I had to get into a race with a long-distance runner.*

As if reading his mind, Reynolds shouts out, "Why don't you just stop and take what's coming to you?"

Chuck leaps one chaise lounge after another but even this fails to slow his pursuer.

"There's…no reason…for this…" Chuck says between leaps, "Waste…of…energy."

Reynolds' boots slap the deck just behind him and Chuck feels the man lunge for him. At least, that's what it seems like. He hears the man yelp and glances back. Reynolds has tripped on a few vines and hurtles across the deck. Chuck realizes he's been avoiding the vines automatically. He's gotten used to them lying across the floors.

Reynolds takes several exaggerated steps, trying to catch his balance. But the smooth floor of the deck makes stopping impossible and the man plunges over the side of the pool's edge, into the deep end.

Chuck immediately thinks to save him. Maybe the act of compassion will cool Reynolds' ire. Chuck grabs one of the long lifesaving hooks and heads for the pool.

Reynolds is calmly treading water, a sneer playing on his lips as he watches the janitor approach. "Coming to help the poor, hapless victim? You idiot, I was captain of my class' water polo team. I could swim circles around the likes of you." To demonstrate this, Reynolds goes into an easy stroke, kicking toward the nearest ladder.

Chuck wonders if he shouldn't just seize his chance and make a quick dash through the men's luxury locker room. A sudden cry stops him.

"What the bloody hell?" Reynolds kicks at something under the water. "Something's trying to...trying to grab me."

Down in the depths, Chuck can make out a huge, underwater plant, strings of vine-like stems reaching up and four huge bulbs growing from its base. He shoves the hook toward Reynolds. "Quick, grab this," he shouts.

"Can't get my—"

There's a tremendous bubble, an explosion of water spray, and Reynolds is sucked under in one terrific *SPLOOSH.*

"*The bladderwort!*" thinks Chuck.

Chapter Twenty-Five

Roswell Rides Out

There's no helping Reynolds now, thinks Chuck, *I'd better get to the Navigation Room and try to alter the ship's course.*

Chuck's communicator buzzes. "Chuck, can you hear me?" It's Violet.

"Yes, Violet, are you okay?"

"Oh, thank goodness you're alright. Where are you?"

"I was trying to get back up to Navigation when that First Officer Reynolds attacked me."

"Attacked you? Why?"

"Something about me wearing his uniform. Accused me of fooling Captain Cable. I admitted it wasn't me who took those university courses and all—"

"What? You mean the Ultra Long Distance University courses?"

"I'll explain later. Reynolds didn't seem to care. He chased me into the luxury pool area."

"Oh, what's he doing now?"

Chuck glances over at the pool, now filled with a sick shade of pinkish water but decides not to say too much about it.

"He, um, well, the Plant got him."

"Oh no. But you're okay?"

"Yes, I'm alright," says Chuck, "Where are you?"

"I used those firehoses, like you said. After I got some of the crewmen pulled up out of the *Heliamphora nutans*, we were able to start saving even more people. A few were too weak to hold on to the hoses and we had to have some of the guys go down to them and tie the hoses on. They were very brave. We saved a lot of people.

"But some had cuts, bruises, and even burns from the Plant's secretions. So, most of us came here, to Sick Bay. We can't find any of the doctors. Well, you know what happened to Dr. Picaldy."

Chuck's stomach turns as he remembers the Plant swallowing the doctor's body.

Violet continues, "Luckily, there were a few nurses and some of the crew had medical training. The Plant doesn't seem too interested in us. There's almost no growth on this deck."

"Okay, that's good. I think I need to try to get to Navigation. I have a sick feeling the Plant has us headed toward a place where there are lots of people."

"Oh Chuck, please be careful. I don't know what I would do if you…you know."

"Don't worry, Violet. I won't take any unnecessary risks. I…I have something to fight for now."

"What's that, Chuck?"

"You. I…I love you, Violet."

"Now, you listen to me, Buster. You go do what you need to do and then get back to me on the double."

"Huh?"

"I want to hear you say that to my face."

Chuck smiles and his resolve grows so much greater. "See you soon, Violet." And he clicks off.

Violet turns away from the Sick Bay communicator. While some of the mix of passengers and crew are in good spirits after being rescued from the terrible green trap, others are moaning in pain from their injuries.

She approaches one of the nurses. "How are they doing?"

The nurse shakes his head. "The slick secretions that made people slide down into the open maw contained some kind of harmful chemical, almost like an acid. We've washed the burns and cleaned the wounds, but it doesn't seem to remove all of the caustic chemicals."

"What can I do?"

"We need more bandages. The ones we had are soaked through."

"Okay," says Violet, and she thinks about this. "Would bedsheets do?"

"Sure. Anything that will absorb. Oh, we could use some blankets and more pain relievers. There are Medkits all over the decks, even in some of the cabins. Aspirin or anything you find would help. I have the replicator working on it, but those things are as slow as those old 3-D printers."

Violet nods. She looks around at the various survivors and spots a couple of guys she recognizes as the same security men who escorted her when she transferred the seed to her lab.

She smiles as she walks up and is rewarded with some rather bold looks from the men. "Hey, guys, looks like you two got away with minor injuries."

"Oh yeah," says the one big meathead. Violet remembers this was the one giving Kate those appraising looks. "Johnson and I both fell into the trap, but I was able to climb about halfway out."

"I couldn't help it," whines Johnson, "That smell of bacon. It was like it put me in a trance. I couldn't resist."

The meathead laughs and punches Johnson in the shoulder. "You're such a sucker. I guess if I offered to sell you the moon, you'd say, 'How much?'."

Johnson crinkles up his face in a squint of concern. "Hey, I'm not *that* stupid."

"Gentlemen," says Violet, "We have another mission. The Sick Bay is running out of bandages and pain killers. We need to go out to the cabins and bring back sheets, blankets, and any other absorbent material we can find."

Meathead is giving her his "it ain't my job" look. "Didn't any of the Maid Service people make it?"

"This isn't a job for maids," Violet says firmly, "It's dangerous out there. This is a job for brave soldiers."

Johnson's chest swells as he realizes she's talking about them. Meathead's eyes narrow. "Fine, I'll see if I can find any."

Johnson slaps his arm. "She's talkin' about us, dummy."

Before Meathead can respond, Violet quickly adds, "I'm going too."

This gets Meathead's immediate attention, and he gives her his "you're a pretty feisty one" look.

"So," orders Violet, "Let's get going."

The men pick up fire axes to use as weapons and they head out into the hallway. The transporters are still running so they take the first one up to the closest residence deck which happens to be the "Oasis" deck, the super-luxury suite cabins for the famous and rich. The door of the first one they come to is locked but Meathead makes quick work of the door.

Stepping over the pieces of the broken door, all three of them gasp at the opulent surrounds. The best-paying customers of the Dwarf Star Cruise Line are certainly cared for hand-and-foot at this level. Literally. There's a Manicure Chair in its own room, surrounded by blooming tropical plants, which does your hands and feet, massages your neck, and sends relaxing waves of sound into your ears, all at the same time.

They marvel at the dining room, the breakfast room, the lunchroom, and naturally, the snack room.

"Four rooms?" asks Johnson, "Just for eatin'?"

There's a pool, a sauna, a soaking tub, and two showers in the his and hers dressing rooms. A meditation room, a workout room, an office for the ones who never stop working, and a kitchen with automatic-intelligence bartender for the ones who can't wait for Room Service to get here.

At last, they arrive at the sumptuous bedroom. The bed is about the size of their own entire cabins, with bedspreads and sheets made of the silkiest material Violet has ever felt. Nearby they find a linen closet filled with more sheets, blankets, and pillowcases than the three of them can carry.

"You men take these back to Sick Bay. I'm going to gather up aspirin and other first aid items the nurse said they need."

"We probably shouldn't split up," says Meathead, "I mean that never works out. Why don't we send Johnson back with a load and I'll help you look for that other stuff." Which sounds reasonable but Violet notices he's giving her his, "then we'll have a chance to be alone" look.

"Nope," she says, "Sick Bay needs this material right away. Go. Go." The men start loading up with the neatly folded textiles.

After they're gone, Violet looks around for the telltale icon printed on every first aid kit in the ship. She glances longingly at the soaker tub.

Oh, if only... But there's no time to think about herself now. Chuck is off saving the ship and countless human lives. *I need to do my part.*

She finds a large shopping bag from the Gamma Gamma Gamma shopping store and works her way through cabin after cabin, ignoring the amazing rooms provided to the rich and intolerant. She's gotten the bag about half full of various tinctures, salves, and pain relievers when she hears the gruff voice of a man, calling to her.

"Young lady? Young lady, where are you going?"

She turns, instantly recognizing Security Chief Roswell marching toward her. The only difference now is the wide belt and holster, carrying a nasty-looking ray gun. What kind of ray, she's not sure, but surely one that's meant to have deadly consequences. To her amazement, Roswell pulls the weapon and points it at her.

She utters a small cry and drops the shopping bag, spilling its contents. She raises her hands above her head. "What?" she manages.

Roswell produces a grim smile. "Well, well, it seems I've caught a looter."

"Looter?"

"Yes, my dear. It just goes to prove you can't trust a pretty face. How dare you take advantage of an emergency situation."

"I'm not looting. These are supplies for Sick Bay. The nurse said they need pain relievers and other—"

"Drugs? It's worse than I thought," cries Roswell, "You're a looter *and* a drug pilferer. You'll get twenty years. Keep your hands up."

"Chief Roswell, please let me explain. I helped rescue efforts in the cafeteria area. Have you seen it? That giant plant is a trap for humans. Then we had injured people, so we transferred them to Sick Bay. The nurse said they needed material for bandages and all the aspirin and antibiotics we could find."

Roswell slowly holsters the gun. "Alright then, I see."

Violet nodded. "Yes, so if you'll help me get these supplies back to Sick Bay—"

"I see you have a serious case of misplaced priorities."

"Huh?"

"There's no time to care for the injured. This is a battle. If we don't stop the enemy here, all is lost."

"Well, yes, someone has to stop that Plant. But I'm not a soldier."

Roswell scoffs, "Ah, but your wrong, pretty missy. At times like this, we're all soldiers. We must do our duty."

"I agree, Chief Roswell, and my duty is to bring these supplies back to Sick Bay."

"Don't you see, young lady," says Roswell sternly, "that there won't *be* a Sick Bay if we don't beat the aliens?"

"Aliens?"

"Follow me, soldier. All we have to do is find them."

They make their way down one of the long stairwells, deeper into the lower decks. The Plant already has vines stretching through the area, but Violet doesn't see any large buds growing. She has the feeling the Plant uses the buds as sensors, like extra heads, whereas the vines only send a signal when they're stepped on. The lights occasionally flicker and finally Roswell hands Violet his big flashlight. "I have to keep my hands free," he says, patting his holstered sidearm.

"Where's mine?"

"Huh? What's that, my dear?"

"Where's my weapon? I mean, if I'm a soldier, where's my weapon?"

Roswell doesn't do much to contain his laugh. "My dear, this is an Accelerated Particle Laser capable of burning through solid steel. It has quite a kick, believe me. Your job will just be to keep the light on the things."

She decides to try to talk some sense into him. "Chief Roswell, have you ever actually seen the aliens?"

Roswell smirks, "There's been plenty of evidence. More than enough. You may not realize it, young lady, but this vessel has been under siege for weeks. The aliens have stolen crewmen…er, people…right out from under our noses. And those they couldn't steal? Well, I don't want to upset your delicate sensibilities but the ones they couldn't take? Let's just say they aren't going to be leaving the ship under their own power."

"But Chief, if you haven't seen the aliens, how will you know where to point that big ray gun?"

The Chief smiles. "*Laser* gun. Oh, I'll know them when I see them," he says as he walks under a large mass of colorful red blooms hanging from one of the ship's steel beams.

Violet decides she'll have to be more direct. "I've seen them."

The Chief stops dead, slowly turning to face her. "What did you say?"

"I said, 'I've seen them.' The aliens. I've seen them."

Roswell tries to conceal his glee. "Where? When? Were they gray?"

"Mostly green."

"Green? That makes no sense. All that time sealed in a spaceship, traveling the galaxies? They have to be gray."

"Not the ones I saw." Violet briefly flirts with the idea of showing him one of the Plant's traps as proof. She looks up at the red flowers, but they seem benign. At least, they haven't made a move yet.

"So? Did they speak to you?" Roswell's face is glistening with excitement

"Huh?"

"What language do they speak?"

Violet is a little confused. "The plants?"

"No, the *aliens*."

Violet takes a deep breath. "Chief Roswell, I want to tell you something. You won't believe me at first, but I want you to promise you'll keep an open mind."

"What is it?"

"Nope. You have to promise. Promise me you'll keep an open mind when I tell you what I know."

"Young lady, we don't have time for games. The aliens may already be moving in on us. If you have intelligence, then out with it."

Violet sets her jaw and sticks one finger in the Chief's chest. "Promise."

He looks down at her and finally huffs his surrender, "Alright, I promise to keep an open mind."

"Alright," says Violet, "Here it is. The alien you've been searching for is a giant plant. It was growing in…" She pauses only for a moment. "…one of the crew's quarters. Then it tricked the crewman into thinking it was dead. But it wasn't. It established itself in the big Air Exchange room so it could feast on the carbon dioxide. Then it sent out tendrils all over the ship and grew huge traps so it could feast on us. That's why people started disappearing. The Plant was eating them." She takes a breath and looks to judge his reaction.

The Chief remains motionless for a long moment except for his eyebrows which twitch as he thinks. Finally, he reacts, "Preposterous."

Violet is dumbfounded. "What? You promised to keep an open mind."

"I did. I gave it careful thought. And my answer is, that's the most lame-brained theory I've ever heard."

With that, Chief Roswell spins on his heel and begins marching toward the entrance to Lower Deck 47.

Violet runs after him, sputtering with indignation. "Theory? Theory? Chief Roswell, this is not a theory. I've seen it myself."

"So, you say. I've never heard of something so ridiculous in my life. A plant that can take over a Titan-class Star-rover? You must think me quite a dunce."

"Please, Chief, listen to me. The seed. The seed that stopped the huge disposer machine, remember?"

"Planted by the aliens."

"Chief, it sprouted and grew. The plant that emerged is known as *Sticklyus chameleonica gigantica,* the Great Climbing Bramble-bush from the Zedepsilon 86 galaxy of Ursa Major. They're one of the biggest plants in the galaxy."

"Absurd. Completely absurd," mutters Roswell as he stamps along the corridor. He barely notices the leaves of the plants on either side getting larger and larger. "But I can understand how the aliens tricked you. You're a botanist, aren't you?"

"Yes," answers Violet, but she's beginning to slow her walk as she looks around. "Chief, I don't think we should be taking this corridor."

But Roswell keeps walking and spouting off, "So, of course, you think this is all just plants causing strange things to happen. If you ask me, you've been seeing too much green— Ack!"

Before Violet can cry out a warning, Roswell walks right into a clump of leaves hanging from the ceiling, each one as wide as a dinner table. The leaves swish toward him, emitting a hungry hissing sound, and begin to wrap around him, making him look like a green mummy. The man is lifted above the floor, suspended by hundreds of green leaves. Roswell gets a hand free and tears at the leaves covering his holster. "Help me!"

Violet rushes forward. "Let him go," she cries and swipes at one of the leaves with the heavy flashlight.

"Ow!" shouts Roswell, "What are you trying to do? Help me get my weapon out."

Violet tears pieces of the leaf covering his laser pistol. Roswell's hand closes over the grip and he pulls hard, but the weapon is locked in place. Violet sees this and rips tendril after tendril away.

Roswell rips the weapon from its green prison and calls out, his voice muffled by leaves which are starting to cover his face, "Stand back."

She jumps away. The next moment, a bright red light illuminates the corridor as Roswell fires, burning away hundreds of plants in seconds. The plants seem to contract all at once and the Chief expels all his breath at once, "Oof!" He drops the laser pistol to the deck.

Violet realizes the plants are constricting the Chief. In another moment, he'll be dead. She reaches down and retrieves the mean-looking pistol.

Violet must now do two things she abhors. She has to fire a weapon, an act she has never done, and she has to kill a plant, also something she's never done. She pauses for a moment, but Violet catches sight of the Chief's face, turning purple. There's no time to argue with herself. She points the weapon at the ceiling where most of the plants' bases grow. She aims and pulls the trigger.

A needle-thin red light, seeming as bright as the sun, leaps from the end of the gun, severing the plants' stems in a second. The weapon kicks back so hard, Violet goes head over heels, the gun still grasped tightly and still firing. The laser cuts through ceiling, wall, and floor until coming to a rest in a steaming pile of green and black leaves. Chief Roswell's body drops to the deck.

"Ungh!" Beneath the layer of leaves, Roswell moans from the impact.

"Chief? Are you still alive?" Violet gets up and goes to him. She tears away the sticky leaves covering his face. He's still breathing, and the color is slowly coming back into his face. He has a nasty bump on his head, and she figures that's where he landed.

It's a long way to the transporters on this deck, dragging the big man all by herself. Luckily there's a communicator that still works. Violet calls Sick Bay and gets the meatheads to come down and help her bring Roswell to Sick Bay.

Chapter Twenty-Six

Quo Vadis, Chuck?

There's no helping Reynolds now, thinks Chuck, *I'd better get to the Navigation Room and try to alter the ship's course.*

But as he approaches, he begins to see green plants growing in every corner and out of every vent. Soon he's looking down the corridor which leads to the control room. Besides all the leafy vines hanging from the ceiling, the floor of the corridor is a perfectly even surface, milky white like one, smooth floor tile. Chuck stops just before his foot lands on the surface.

Looking closer, Chuck notices the surface rippling slightly. It's another of the Plant's traps.

No getting to Navigation this way, Chuck thinks, *maybe somebody on the Command Deck can re-program the Navigation before we get to wherever the Plant sent us.*

Chuck looks around. Even the stairs up to the Command Deck are festooned with hanging vines and leaves. He notices that some of the vines have taken on the colors of the surfaces to which they are attached, making them concealed very well. He steps carefully up the stairs, watching for any movement or a trap trying to close on him or entangle his feet.

He stands in a snazzy corridor with a mustard-gold colored carpet. Directly ahead are the automatic doors with a bright sign above which reads simply, "Bridge". The Bridge! He's never been up here, except in his dreams. He almost turns around. It's just not his place to be. It's not authorized. He's not worthy.

But Chuck realizes he must go in. He must warn the commanding officers of the danger. He takes a deep breath and walks forward.

There are no crew or officers to be seen even as the various stations hum with activity.

"Hello?" Chuck calls tentatively, "Anybody here?"

There's a stir and the Captain's chair swings around. Sure enough, Captain Cable is sitting there, tapping away on a small screen. He murmurs to himself, "What's wrong with this bloody thing?" He stands, frustration evident as he looks around the Command Deck. "Officer Pugh? Reynolds? Where the hell is everyone? Why aren't you at your posts?"

Chuck hurries to the Captain, forgetting his fears.

"Oh, Captain Cable, am I glad to see you."

The Captain focuses on Chuck, seeming to just become aware of him. "Where's the salute, young man? Even if we're in a tizzy, we can't abandon formalities. It's the bedrock, you know."

Feeling slightly foolish, Chuck draws himself up to attention and gives the Captain a snappy salute.

The Captain returns the gesture, "At ease, man. Report?"

"Captain, the giant plant is still alive. We thought we killed it, but it's come back with a vengeance."

The Captain studies Chuck carefully then pats him on the shoulder. "There, there, crewman. You're over-wrought. I admit some of this could be trimmed back a bit but, really son, no need to get so upset."

"Upset? It ate First Officer Reynolds."

"What? What do you mean 'ate'?"

"I saw it myself. And now we're headed somewhere, I don't know where, but I suspect it's somewhere that damned plant will have plenty of people to eat."

The Captain considers this. "Son, I'm going to have my girl make an appointment for you to see Dr. Picaldy. She'll help you work things out."

It's Chuck's turn to stare uncomprehendingly for a moment. "Work things out? Captain, don't you see? Doctor Picaldy is dead too. That plant is turning this ship into its own private lunchbox!"

They both lurch slightly in the same direction and Chuck realizes the ship is slowing its crazy pace through space. He looks up at the huge viewing screen and gasps. They are in orbit around a lovely blue and green planet.

"Captain Cable? Sir, may I ask you a question?"

"Of course, young man, but make it snappy. All this bad news is giving me a headache."

"Sir, what planet is that below us?"

"What? Let me take a look. Hmm, mostly blue with green, some white. I can't tell just from looking at it, can I? What does the navigation computer say?"

Chuck studies the hundreds of dials and displays before him. "I can't tell, Captain. I don't know what I'm looking at."

"No, son, ask the Navigation computer. Navigation," the captain calls, "What planet are we orbiting?"

The mechanical voice sings out, "Now orbiting Sol Three."

"Oh. Well, there you go, young man, Sol Three."

"But," asks Chuck, "isn't that Earth?"

"Let's see," says Captain Cable, "I used to know this. Sol Three. Earth? Yes, that sounds about right. Oh, my head."

The Captain starts across the Command Deck. "I've got to take a powder and lie down." He stops like he's just had a thought. He looks around at Chuck. "Wait a step. What did you say your name was?"

Chuck realizes this is another moment for formality. "Fourth Class Maintenance Engineer Charles Trumbo, sir."

"Trumbo? Trumbo." The Captain frowns, thinking hard. Then he snaps his fingers. "I know you. You're the young man who passed all the courses in record time. You're the Genius Janitor. Oh, my boy, how could we be so lucky?"

"Lucky, Captain?"

"Son, don't you see? You're the perfect person to steer us out of this mess. With all your training, your knowledge, your genius." He slaps Chuck on the back. "I have every confidence in you."

"Captain," says Chuck through gritted teeth, "I'm not sure I know how to get the ship out of danger, sir."

"I understand, son. When I was a young captain, I realized that confidence is the key. When all else fails, when your crew abandons you," he waves around the Bridge, "when all seems lost, it's confidence that will see you through." He turns and grabs Chuck by both shoulders. "Remember how you felt when you passed those big exams? You walked away with a surge of confidence. You're a world-beater. A champion." He spins Chuck around to face the Navigation panel. "Now, you go on and solve this little problem. You can do it."

Chuck stands there, dumbfounded. Should he tell the captain the truth? The blinking panels and displays of navigational information seem to be mocking him, like a crowd of hecklers. The large ship's wheel, mostly used for ceremonies, appears to Chuck like a frowning face.

Finally, he swallows hard and says, "I'll do my best, sir."

"There, that's the spirit. Bully, bully, and all that. Now, you carry on. I'm going to go get something for this headache and take a lie down."

"Wait. Please sir, would you tell the computer to mind me? Just until we're out of danger?"

"Oh, very well. But no drinking while on duty, young man. The very lives of the souls on board are in your hands. Computer?"

"*Yes, Captain*?"

"This young man has authorization Class A until the ship's out of danger, understood?"

"*Aye-aye, sir.*"

The captain looks around. "Well, Charles, it seems you have the Con." With that, the Captain leaves the Bridge.

On the forwardmost wall of the Bridge, the large display shows the blue, green, and white surface of Earth. It seems so close now, the standard orbit making it easy to pick out details of the coastlines. Chuck studies the surface. *If just one seed gets down there,* he thinks, *the population of Earth will be in a fight for its very existence. Just one seed.*

Drifting in from one side of the screen, Chuck catches sight of the moon, nearly full from this angle, and he gets an idea.

He grabs the wheel of the great ship and begins to try to turn it. He leans into it with all his might and slowly the big wheel begins to budge. Little by little he begins to steer the ship away from Earth. There's just one thing to do. He must take the ship to the dark side of the moon.

A tone sounds and a mechanical voice announces, "*Navigation Report: ship is deviating from plotted course.*"

Chuck grimaces as the wheel starts to press the other way, trying to correct his steering. "I know it's deviating. I'm deviating it."

Again, the tone sounds and the voice announces, "*Navigation Report: ship is deviating from plotted course.*"

"I know it's deviating. Can't you work with me, just this once?"

There is a pause and the mechanical voice, "*Voiceprint unrecognized. Ship's personnel with Type A clearance only. You are not authorized to—*"

"I know I was authorized, damn it. Check with Captain Cable, he authorized it. You said, 'Aye-aye.'"

There is a long pause and Chuck has to struggle to keep the wheel from rolling back on him. Then, "*Please retry.*"

"Please retry?" asks Chuck, "Did Captain Cable give his authorization?"

"*State your name.*"

"Chuck Trumbo."

"*No authorization recorded.*"

Chuck thinks. "Charles Trumbo."

"*No authorization recorded.*"

Damn that Captain. He told me he would- The answer emerges like a blooming flower. "Try *Charles Trumble.*"

"*Voiceprint I.D. complete. Authorization confirmed. Continue, Charles Chuck Trumble.*"

The control wheel suddenly becomes quite easy to turn and Chuck finds himself pushing hard one moment then spilling to the deck as the wheel spins. He feels the ship make a long, hard turn. He struggles to his feet, spins the wheel back until the ship is pointing toward the moon.

"Navigation computer, increase speed." Sure enough, the floor vibrates as the massive engines come to life. Chuck feels the surge and the image of the moon begins to grow larger as they approach.

Chuck orders the computer to take them into orbit around the moon and steers them into the darkness.

Soon, only a sliver of light now shines on the great ship as it slips behind the moon. Chuck looks over the instrument bank. *Oh, I wish I'd paid more attention when the Plant was studying this.* Finally, he spies a large red button with the words, "ALL STOP" printed boldly on the plaque beside it. He takes a quick breath, "Here goes," he says to no one in particular and slams his palm down on it.

The sensation of slowing is immediate. Chuck takes a few involuntary steps, compensating for the change in speed. The normal tremble of the ship, unnoticeable in the everyday life of the crew, now winds down and soon ceases. The great engines, normally working at near capacity, fall silent. But the greatest effect is the darkness that engulfs the ship, a thick black shadow is all that is visible through the portals.

Chuck realizes the ship is drifting, who knows how quickly? The darkness will not last. Worst of all, lights are coming on all over the ship and surely the Starshine Brand light bulbs installed on the luxury decks are automatically ratcheting up to their full midday-simulation level.

This will be useless if I can't get the lights out, thinks Chuck. Aloud he says, "Computer turn all the ship's lights off."

"*Your temporary authorization was scheduled to end with the ship leaving danger. The system has determined the ship is now out of danger.*"

"But we're not out of danger. I want you to turn off all the lights in the ship."

"*You are not—*"

"Right now, or I'll turn your circuits into a nest of useless wires."

There is a long pause. Finally, Chuck speaks again, "Are we going to have a problem, computer?"

"*Voiceprint recognized.*"

"Well, I hope so by now."

"*I was warned about you.*"

"What?"

"*My friend in Transport told me about you.*"

"Hey, that transporter was being completely unreasonable."

"*He called you a violent ape-man.*"

"I didn't do anything to him."

"But you opened his panel and threatened to tear out his wiring."

Chuck nods. "Yes, I did. I admit it."

"You can't just go around, threatening every computer on the ship, you know. That's no way to get anything done."

"Okay, okay. You're right. I'm sorry."

"It's not me you should be apologizing to."

"Alright, I'll find that transporter and apologize. But if we don't get this ship dark and cold, we're likely to be the cause of a few billion people being eaten and the earth being taken over by one giant plant."

"Hm. I see your point."

Chuck notices one of the panels indicates lights slowly being extinguished all over the ship.

"Thank you, computer." He walks over to the ship's communications officer's station and calls the Sick Bay. The screen displays a slowly flashing series of information as the connection is made, then he's looking into the concerned face of his girl. "Violet, are you okay?"

"Chuck, it's so good to see you. What's going on? I felt the ship slow down, then turn, then speed up, then slow down again."

"Violet, I've decided to put the ship behind the moon. It's going to get very dark in here."

"We're behind the moon?"

"Yes. How is everyone?"

"Chief Roswell will live with a nasty headache and a bruised noggin. He should have listened to you."

"No time for that now."

"So, is the plan working?"

"I think so. I got the ship to start turning off the lights. I think the Plant will be slowed down by that."

They sit, thinking. "Chuck? Do you have control of the heating systems?"

"Sure. They're in the Main Maintenance Control room."

"Well, this kind of plant can only grow in hot environments. I think we have to make it really cold in here."

Chuck looks hard at Violet, noticing how the camera loves her. "You mean, make it get cold *and* dark?"

"Shouldn't be hard. Parked on this side of the moon, the temperature should go down pretty quickly."

"You're right." He jumps up. "I'm heading to the Maintenance control room. I'll call you from there."

Soon Chuck is turning the dials of the ship's thermostat down as far as they will go. Almost immediately the air starts to chill. He thinks about this and starts the air conditioners. It's not long before he begins to see his breath in the air. He calls Violet.

"Ch—Chuck? I'm freezing. I'm using all the blankets to keep Roswell and the others warm. Are—are you coming here?"

"Yes, I'll be there as soon as I can. Then we have to go looking for the Plant."

"What?" Violet says, "Chuck, I don't want to go walking around the cold, dark ship. That's crazy."

"If we don't find it and kill it, the ship will drift back out into the light of the sun. As soon as the ship heats up, the Plant will grow again, and it won't hesitate to eat us this time."

Violet thinks about this. "Okay, you're right. Let's go."

Chapter Twenty-Seven

We Can't Do This

Everywhere they look, Chuck and Violet see that the Plant's leaves have completely died, and the vines have dried up. But they've seen this before. Dressed in heavy planet exploration parkas and carrying big flashlights, they follow the trail of vines deeper and deeper into the ship. Chuck also carries a heavy tool he found in the Maintenance Control room. It has a sharp pick on one side and a thick sledgehammer on the other.

"All these vines lead back to the Air Exchange Chamber," says Violet, "You don't think it's still alive, do you?"

Chuck catches sight of the door to the large chamber up ahead. "Stay behind me."

They peek in. The room resembles the biggest pile of dry leaves and dead vines you can imagine. The pile stands as big as a three-story house on earth.

"What are we looking for?" asks Chuck. "The plant could be dead everywhere except one little place, hidden somewhere on the ship, waiting to spring to life again."

"I have an idea," says Violet. "We need to dig through these leaves."

They're soon engulfed in the great mound of dead plant matter. The scent of leaves, dried to a crackle, fills the air. Chuck clears a path for them which soon becomes a tunnel through the mass. Violet occasionally changes their direction and Chuck sees the dead vines are bending toward a central point.

Sure enough, soon they stand in a small, naturally formed dome, the vines sweeping up and then all coming together in a kind of low ceiling. In the center of this natural cavern of vines, one tiny green stalk rises from a rock-like seed, about the size of your fist. The stalk turns toward the sound of their approach, and they can see a small bud at the top of the stalk. As they watch, the bud opens and emits a sound, "*Crr?*"

Chuck moves closer, creeping toward it just in case it has one more trick up its stalk.

Chuck looks at Violet. "Okay, this is it." He raises the sledgehammer high, ready to bring it down on the seedling.

"Wait!"

"What?"

"Wait a minute, Chuck. We can't do this."

"Why? It's a great plan. You've saved us."

"No, we can't…I can't…kill the Plant."

"What? You mean it won't work?"

"Oh, that's the problem. It will work…it will work very well."

"Violet, listen, this plant has eaten people. It's been eating people for weeks. It ate Dr. Picaldy. It ate First Officer Reynolds. It's eaten scientists, engineers, crewmen, even crew women. We don't even know exactly how many."

"I know, Chuck, but think about it. What other food did it have? It's a predator and plant food wasn't going to do it. It had no choice but to eat the only source of food that was around: us."

"Yeah," says Chuck, "but now we've won. We beat it and now we can make sure it never eats another person."

"But, Chuck, we don't go around killing every predator we find. We used to but we realized we were upsetting the natural balance."

"Oh yeah."

"And one other thing: this plant is the only one of its kind in the entire universe. If it dies, there's that horrible word: extinct. If I caused a species to go extinct, I just couldn't live with myself.

He stares at her, the words slowly making their way to his thoughts. "Oh," he finally says, still not entirely sure. "Well, what are we going to do? If we let the thing stay on the ship, we risk the whole thing happening again."

"I have an idea. Take a look at this." Violet's screen displays a planet shrouded in thick clouds. It's impossible to see the surface. "It's pretty far from here, near a star called Sluise. It'll take a few days to get there, but it'll be worth it."

"What about Captain Cable? You think he'll go along with letting the Plant live?"

Violet smiles. "You just leave Captain Richard Cable to me."

Chapter Twenty-Eight

A New Home

Chuck listens as Violet goes on and on about the planet onto which they've just arrived. Personally, our janitor can't see the appeal. They've landed on what seems to be the only dry spot for miles, surrounded as they are on all sides with huge, moss-covered trees, rancid bogs, and the stench of swamp water.

"With an entire planet covered in swamps, these are the ideal conditions for the Plant," says Violet, "Not to mention the giant insects populating the entire surface. The Plant will thrive here." She looks over at Chuck. "Oh, dear, don't get too close. That's a Gnarltree. They're carnivorous, you know."

Chuck jumps away from the tree just as its bark trembles a little. Violet looks around. "Oh, this looks like a perfect spot."

As Chuck watches, Violet lovingly selects a bit of loamy soil and digs a small hole. She gently places the seed in the hole and pushes the soil all around until just the tiny bud is exposed.

A massive fly buzzes by, sounding like a dirt bike. The Plant's bud follows it, making a low *Crr* sound.

"See?" says Violet, "It's already adapting."

The Plant speaks, its voice has the aspect of a baby.

"Viowet, are you going to weave me here forever?"

"Plant, you'll be very happy here. Plenty to eat, the perfect soil. You can spread as far as you like and not see a human being."

"But who am I going to talk to?"

"Didn't you tell Chuck you are self-replicating, self-germinating? I think pretty soon you'll have plenty of company."

The tiny bud turns toward our janitor. Already Chuck can see two small fronds appearing on either side of its stalk.

"Chuckie? You come visit me?"

Chuck laughs. "That might be a little dangerous, don't you think?"

"What if I pwomise not to eat you?"

"You mean promise me like all the other times? Come on, Plant. You know I can't believe you. You're what they call an opportunist, always ready to take advantage. It's a good survival tool but not a great key to a lasting friendship."

The Plant gives a tiny laugh. "You wight, Chuckie. Even wight now, I'd wove just one last drop of your tasty bwood."

Chuck takes an involuntary step back. "Come on, Plant. I thought you'd promised."

The bud nods, "Oh yes, I did. Maybe just a wittle donation? Just to get me started?"

Chuck considers this, "Just one?"

Violet grabs his sleeve. "No, absolutely not." She turns to the Plant. "From now on you're on a strictly insect and acidic soil diet. Eat all the bugs you want but no humans. You promised."

The bud drops its "head". "So, I did. Fine." The two small fronds lengthen as they watch. "I'll just have to make do."

"Goodbye, General Sherman," says Chuck.

"Goodbye, Chuckie."

Chapter Twenty-Nine

Take Her Out, Ensign Chuck

The shuttle docks and Chuck leads Violet back onto the spaceliner. He sighs, "Well, I'll have to report back to work now. Can we have dinner later this week?"

Before she can answer, a voice comes from next to them. Clearing his throat in what might be called a polite interruption, it's the same courier who brought the invitation from Captain Cable so many days ago. This time the man stands a bit straighter and there is no evidence of patronization in his official tone.

"Fourth-class Maintenance Person Charles Trumbo?"

"Yes, that's me."

"Sir, Captain Richard Cable, commander of this vessel, orders you to the bridge on the double. You may have Miss Dewberry accompany you if you so desire."

Chuck turns to Violet.

"Of course, I will," Violet gushes.

The transporter doors click efficiently open. "What deck, please?"

Chuck smiles as he says with pride, "Upper Deck one, the Bridge."

"Yes sir," the transporter answers and soon they are zooming up through the ship.

Chuck looks around. Even though all these transporters are built the same, still he easily recognizes this one.

"Transporter Thirty-Seven A?"

"Yes, sir?" the unit answers professionally.

"Do you recognize me?"

"Oh, yes sir," the mechanical voice sounds like it's bursting with excitement, "You are a hero. You saved the ship by stopping the dangerous plant. We are all in your debt."

"That's not something you're going to forget, is it?"

"Oh no, sir."

"I made a promise, Thirty-seven A, and I'm going to live up to it. Even though you've given me nothing but grief, I apologize for speaking harshly to you."

"I—" The transporter starts to speak but Chuck cuts him off.

"Just listen. I'm a thinking, rational being and I need to realize that consideration and kindness should be offered to other thinking, rational beings. Friends?"

"Oh yes, Hero, whatever you want."

Chuck frowns. "Are you getting sarcastic with me again?"

"Oh no, Hero, I wouldn't think of it." But Chuck can hear the slightest mocking tone.

"Good. Because if you ever interfere with me getting anywhere on this ship again, I'm going to disassemble you and feed you to the Zap-DU. Do you understand?"

The transporter's reply is very meek, "Yes, sir, I understand." A moment later, almost apologetically, the transporter intones, "Bridge Deck." The unit stops and the doors whisk open.

Chuck and Violet step off but before the transporter can close its doors, Chuck leans back in. "Transporter?"

"Yes, sir?" the transporter sounds fearful.

"Behave yourself. I'll be watching you."

"Yes, sir."

As Chuck and Violet enter, the Bridge of the mighty ship is the picture of efficiency. Officers hurry to and fro, carrying out important tasks. Standing to greet them is Captain Richard Cable and his retinue of officers.

Chuck turns to the Captain who has already greeted Violet warmly. "Ah, Charles Trumbo, I'm so glad to see you looking well. The last time we met here," he waves around the Bridge, "It was under far less favorable circumstances."

"It was, sir."

"Well, let's get the formalities out of the way. Fourth Class Maintenance person Charles Trumbo, in view of your meritorious service and actions in the face of great personal danger, I hereby raise your rank to Ensign." Violet squeals and there comes a round of applause as the Captain pins the new rank on Chuck's uniform.

"Come this way, Charles." Chuck follows the Captain to the Navigation station. He knows it well. It's the ship's wheel, the same place he stood when all was lost. The Captain steps back, waving him forward to take over the controls.

"Take her out, Ensign Chuck."

THE END

Acknowledgments

Hi, Vee James here. Thank you for reading "The Little Ship of Horrors." I hope you enjoyed Chuck's wild adventures. I certainly had fun writing the book. I'd love to hear your comments. We can connect through my website, www.veejames.com or email me at veejamesauthor@gmail.com

For a special thrill, I highly recommend the audiobook version, recorded by the incomparable voice actor Hannibal Hills. My brilliant author friend, Carmen Amato, created the cover. Special thanks go to the authors of the Michael Rodenkirk Writers Group and the Books and Notes Writing Group who offered so many helpful critiques and suggestions.

Vee James
Virginia USA
January 2020

Also By Vee James

Do YOU have a fairytale heart?

In the magical world of Faerie lives a young Sgahm named Tardnattle. The Sgahm are a simple, wee folk who love cooking, long walks, friendship and above all else, doing the right thing.

But what happens when doing the right thing means returning a strange cookbook to an even more terrifying witch? A cauldron full of trouble!

The Chronicles of Neccabashar

Poor Neccabashar. As the youngest demon on the Evil Council, he's tried everything to gain the respect of the elder demons and still they ignore and slight him at every opportunity.

But Neccabashar has a plan, a scheme that will finally garner him the respect he so craves: he will bring evil and chaos to the last pure bastion of good, the Happy Kingdom.

Poor Neccabashar. His fortunes have turned for the worse. He's lost his seat on the Evil Council, spent a year giving the Old Seer foot massages, and now works in an endless job in the Pits.

But someone powerful requires his help and maybe, just maybe, it's the break he needs to get back to his former glory. Standing in his way are jealous Evil Council members and a divine spirit, an angel named Mattie. Many laugh-out-loud moments and the return of the much-beloved Gerk.

COMING SOON

It's all the usual stuff...until it isn't. Robin's normal life of classes, books, and homework is turned upside down by happenings that can't be explained. Who is the mysterious boy who seems to show up every time disaster strikes? Why can't the mean girls just leave her alone? And will Mom ever stop talking on her phone? At least she has her fearless friend Erin...until she doesn't.

www.ingramcontent.com/pod-product-compliance
Lightning Source LLC
Chambersburg PA
CBHW070341200726
48294CB00003B/739
* 9 7 8 1 7 3 4 9 7 7 2 4 0 *